A Short Dance in the Sun

George Benet

The Lapis Press

Venice   San Francisco

A tribute to all the West Coast ILWU *longshoremen,*
clerks, and walking bosses—living and dead

Book design by Les Ferriss.
Cover photo by Mike Vawter.
Text type is Sabon. Digital composition by
Wilsted & Taylor, Oakland, California.

The Lapis Press
589 N. Venice Blvd.
Venice, CA 90291

Distributed by
Publishers Services
PO Box 2510
Novato, CA 94948

ISBN 0-932499-58-9 paper

Contents

1 *A Lonesome $5.00 Room*

It took eight tries to put my pants on. Already weak from the countless spasms that wracked my body, I climbed from the bed and made another attempt. Although I had been in bed the entire long night, I was exhausted.

The room in the Dominic Hotel was as small as a coffin, and that's how I thought of it. In a city of exhilaration and activity, I imagined myself lying dead, a sick, ugly body bloated by booze. The room had a short bed with grey sheets; I never put them out in time to have them changed. The room was large enough for only a narrow passage between the bed and the open closet . . . two dirty shirts and a bulky sweater, gravy and wine stained, that I had borrowed. The one waste basket overflowed with empty orange, grape, and root beer cans and empty bottles of Ballerina and Royal Gate vodka. Dozens of bottles scattered across the floor; many more were shoved into the drawers of the only dresser. One cardboard box, jammed full of papers and clothes. Like my life, the room was in shambles.

The coughing started again, deep in the pit of my stomach, and each cough shook my body—trembling, spasms, tears, gagging. No food to vomit; I hadn't eaten in days. The sweat slick against the dirt of my body, no bath for more than two weeks. Each day I made a promise to bathe, but I was so weak and afraid I would fall in the tub or slip in the shower and lay there with a concussion or a broken leg. And when I was in the Eagle Cafe and had four or five drinks and the shakes subsided and the arrogance returned, I would forget the shower or the bathing. I was unable to smell, but others must gag.

On the eighth try I managed to haul the pants up my legs, my balance so shaky that I fell back on the bed, squirming from side to side to get the pants up. I reminded myself not to take the pants off again. I could not remember, but sometime in the night I must have kicked the pants from my body. Although it was cold outside, the room was stuffy, without a window open for ventilation. My heart pumped like a trip hammer. I had high blood pressure, and I knew it must be astronomical now. I lay on the bed exhausted, my breath in short, wheezing gasps and always on the edge of convulsive coughing.

By raising my head, I could see some small change on the dresser, not much. I felt into my pockets—one bill. Shakily pulling it out and looking, a lonesome five in a lonesome room. Get to the Eagle and cuff some money in a place where my credit was near its limit. Days gone by without recollection. I didn't know what day it was, vaguely remembering borrowing money from the credit union at the hall. I had signed a loan for five hundred dollars and actually received two hundred in cash. The five was all that was left. Weakly raising my head again, I looked around on the floor . . . but no luck. For a gambler who sometimes lived on luck, my luck was miserable. My brother, business agent for our union—the San Francisco Longshoremen—was away at a convention, and his wife was strictly no-tap city as far as I was concerned.

The image of a trapped animal hit me, and with renewed strength I sat on the bed and plowed through the bottles, pouring the dribbles and hoping against hope that one bottle might accidentally hold a shot. Totaled, barely enough to wet my tongue. The blood pressure pills were long gone, and blood pounded in my head. One goal. Get out and get a drink.

Sunday . . . and the only bar open on the waterfront was Riordans'. I sat on a stool, my heels locked in the metal rung. Never had I been so weak, hands trembling, even my knees shaking. They were talking about the night before. A dozen rats had run in through the swinging doors, then over the bar and the bottles to get to the Polish sausages—the customers banging at them with poolsticks, kicking them, blood all over the floor. I tightened my heels on the rungs. I wouldn't have had enough strength to kick them away. Christ, to find an open bar and this bullshit . . . rats.

"How big were they?" I asked.

"Big as dogs," the bartender answered.

He reminded me of an old tintype, hair plastered down, old-fashioned striped shirt. I knew him to be tough. A no-nonsense man who had done time in the joint. Good for a tap if he was in the right mood. Buy drinks out of his own pocket if necessary.

"Since they tore down all the warehouses and piers, they're hungry as tigers." A black postal worker talking.

The bar was primarily for longshoremen, teamsters, and postal workers, plus a collection of winos who filtered in and out . . . never trading over the bar, but coming in for take-out bottles of wine. Just in and out, half-battered and sick-looking men with froggy voices.

"Gimme a vodka and orange juice," I said. "Light on the orange."

The bartender placed the drink before me. "Never have I seen the motherfuckers so bold. One ran clean along the bottles, and I just got out of the way. Looked like a battlefield."

"Any come in today?" I asked. My hands shook as I reached for the drink.

The magic in a few drinks of vodka. The trick was to get the first ones down fast. Spill as little as possible. Get it past the throat without gagging.

"Must of had a rough night," the bartender said, as he watched me suck the drink down. The knowing eyes focused on my bloated face and pudgy hands, fat as pork sausages.

"I'm not too loaded," I said. "Am I good for a tap?"

"Ten bucks, no more. We got bum checks a mile high. The boss said no more checks."

"I don't mean a check."

"I know what you mean, but two of the checks are yours." Rats and checks.

By the fourth drink my hands had calmed, and as I stood to go to the toilet, my legs seemed steadier. But drinking in the bar put me under a double pressure. I didn't want to leave. I had no place to go. People, even friends, were tired of seeing me. Tired of loaning me money or having me drinking all the booze in their houses or talking all that ragtime talk of the good old days. Tired of the old stories, just generally sick and tired of a pest and in some ways a stranger who was on a different circuit that had only one direction . . . down hill. But mainly, I couldn't go back to my room. If I could sleep, it might be okay, but not to lie there and look at the ceiling and four walls of the room that was to be my coffin. The constant vision of my runaway wife. Christ, I couldn't still be drinking over her. We hadn't slept together for the last five years of our marriage, and my last two years were miserable. Maybe a person preferred misery over lonesomeness.

I ordered another drink. I was unstable, overwhelmed with exhaustion. I couldn't remember when I had last eaten. I stunk like a goat. In a place where every other wino stunk like a goat, I was acceptable . . . nowhere else.

I had no money, nothing in the bank, checks bouncing all over the place. I was tap city.

And now I was back in the room, prepared for the silent and paralyzing trip to insanity or destruction. Try as I might, I couldn't say death.

At night I saw the rats. Hard to concentrate on them when the small angels spelled them off in relief. Small angelic girls with pouty girl faces and curly golden hair and straight-up wings attached to their backs.

My wife had been gone for more than twelve years.

The loneliness didn't come right after her departure. No, not until two years ago. We didn't get along, and our last years together were a mess. But the mind can dispel bad memories. When I thought of her recently, it would be an Easter memory. We were on the Marina Green, and my daughter was flying a Japanese kite high in the air. My wife wore a pale lemon-colored dress and a floppy white hat and carried a white parasol. She had legs that were showstoppers, even made old men turn around. We walked hand in hand, and my daughter held my other hand. As we ate, my wife's leg brushed mine, and I knew it was intentional. I lit her cigarettes for her, and the girl blew out the matches. We were together like a communion. Often she lapsed into silence, and her eyes sparkled, and we knew—she knew—I loved her, and I knew she knew. Whatever was in my face and the pressure of my hand on hers told her we were one. The church ceremony that had united us made us one. Our daughter was the product of our love and passion. After we ate in the Basque restaurant, we danced to the accordian player. He played "La Paloma." The girl sucked on a root beer with a straw. The glow in her face responded to our movements as we faked a tango, "La Paloma" over and over again.

A constant flood of images, a merry-go-round. The blanket tight about my neck, constantly shivering with cold, brushing cobwebs from my face. No longer could I tell the imagined from the real. Maybe these images from the past were just as unreal.

My wife was a good dancer, wrote fine poetry, was Portuguese. Her father had been a longshoreman. He was dead, in Holy Cross Cemetery. I remembered him vaguely on the job, at the wedding his bulky-shouldered pride when he looked at his daughter. Her somber flashing eyes, the slender legs, and the *cara delgada* face . . . and the hair, tarantula black, and the eyes dark as ink. Danced the Greek dances in the Minerva with an impenetrable face, a mask, as she caught the jaunty, lilting rhythm. She had no temper in the early days of our marriage, not even after her first hospitalization. Her sulkiness, her deep, despairing moods increased with her fear of the endless rounds of operations.

After the child was born, she went to a therapist. Our priest suggested it. Until then our sex life had never really been satisfactory—straight sex, one position only, the stiff uptightness of a virgin as she was the day I married her. The original intention, the reason she visited the therapist, was to locate emotionally, psychologically, the cause of her severe headaches. But after each visit to the therapist, I found a new woman in her bed. Unerringly, after each session, kinky stuff, often masochistic. I asked no questions, and she gave no answers. Her ability to wear black and white underclothes with a mood of wild passion.

After her therapy visits started, her headaches were no longer a point of discussion between us. We went to mass every Sunday, and finally I quit wondering . . . how can you do anything wrong with your own wife? And then she stopped wearing underclothes, and when I came home I would shower, and we followed the ritual of dinner, kisses on the couch while the child watched TV. Then the late nights and wild shatterings! Her lips were sensual and soft, and her teeth nippy as she consumed me alive. I could hardly watch her nibble asparagus without getting a hard-on. Her cooking improved during that time.

The nights we spent trout fishing, camping out, and lying in our sleeping bags on cots. She listened in silence as I pointed out the constellations to the girl, Orion, Cassiopeia. And the sunsets at the beach, caressing and rolling in the surf. The time under the trees in Muir Woods during the monumental rainstorm when my blue blazer shrunk. The Marina Green with my stroking atop her, barely hidden from the arcs of the commuter headlights going toward the bridge. I whispered, "This is insanity. We have a house and a bed only four blocks away!"

We turned each other on. No whips or tying up or swinging arrangements with other couples; none of that bullshit. Just the expansion of our love into the physical.

And the ribbings I got from my brother. "Don't you ever go out and play cards on Fridays anymore?" I had been a great gambler, horseplayer, cardplayer. "People will think you're square, going to the ball games and the racetrack with your own wife. She must have the best-looking legs in the whole goddam city, but Jesus Christ, you two will burn each other out."

We did, but it took a long time. The epileptic dances in the late night became kinkier, but all that was noticeable, except to my brother, was our love. She was a nontalker, silent as a tomb, and I volunteered no information.

The rats and the little girl angels were back again, along with the snakes and the explanations needed if I was to keep from going insane. Maybe not eating, no food made me dizzy in the brain and unable to stay with a single thought. Generally alcohol erased the blackboard of my mind, scattering the past into broken pieces to be tossed from the bridge into suicides of floating paper that kept me from going off the bridge on my own. Should I write a note in the darkness, explaining what I am to do, if I'm sure of what I'm about to do?

Two more drinks. The earlier ones were harder to get down, and these with strawberry soda from the small fridge in the corner— vodka and soda, how crazy can I get? What about the rats and the angels and the snakes and the tattoos and the visions of my wife's black panties and none of my dad who died in a mine accident in the Mother Lode? And my mom, with her heavy way of walking, buried up the hill in Jackson, and dad deep in the mine locked in with whatever secrets transpired in the carbon darkness. Never the figure of my wife, never Maria Teresa herself. The entire feel of her as a presence, some gypsy-conjured mood, some vodka-induced trance glimpsed from the corner of my eye. Never sure, sometimes terrifying, the longshoremen, the living mixed with the dead, floating heads bobbing alongside the ships, squashed by vans falling from cranes, and heads torn asunder. Asunder, I don't even know the word *asunder*. The vast army of the dead crowding the corners of the room. Repeat after me . . . a hallucination is a temporary dysfunction of the reticular networklike activating mechanism of the brainstem. Images that don't belong together are brought together. A hallucination is exaggerated by apprehension. What am I apprehensive about? Apprehensions are unnamed fears, and what are mine? Certainly not death or my divorced wife or the waterfront. And I'm not afraid of love or rejection or hate or resentment or even self-pity, for that matter. Why snuff out life? The lack of hope? To awaken and face a bleak and despairing landscape each day.

I was not an existential being, not a child of those dark, moody philosophers or even novelists or Doctor Menninger's dictum: Drinking is a form of suicide, a vicious circle. One drinks to ease the pain of despair and not to commit suicide, and drinking lulls me. What does Menninger know about black friction tape placed over the windows with trembling fingers to shut out the light of life, and how the room might be a dim tunnel like a mine or a coffin or associated with the blackness of a woman's hair, and what did I have left of her but a few pubic hairs in the wallet behind the driver's license, and how nutty can one get? Black tape darkness mine tunnel coffin hair Maria Teresa despair unnamed fears that may or may not be self-perpetuating and cause apprehension. I know I am in reality, and the visions do not make much sense, and they are not uncomfortable unless they are terrifying. And how could my dad or Maria Teresa be terrifying? And why continual flood of sensual memories? How strange now, when I rarely thought about that part of our life and was not a victim of fantasy or did not overdream . . . was this all a dream? My spasms started again, and when I was not able to control the coughing and the retching, the shuddering of the body into convulsions, I knew that this was no dream.

One way of clearing my mind, stopping the merry-go-round of would-haves, should-haves, could-haves, might-have-beens . . . pour three or four ounces of vodka or gin into the glass, no need for any ice, pour in some mix, and down the hatch. Feel it go past my throat into my stomach, the warmth and the hit, the spreading contact with all my senses, the deadening of nerves. The periods of reprieve shorter and shorter. Another glassful. Where would it all end? The rats had come up on the bed, and the angels were toying with my hair, and I started to sweat.

Once, getting up from the bed, a complete nothing—senseless for how long? I had fallen on the floor, and my fingers were bruised, and I lay propped against the side of the bed, the front of my pants completely wet. Had I poured booze on me, upset a glass, or was it urine? Did I have a convulsion? Cautiously rising from the floor onto the bed and crawling under the covers, breathing heavy, then the caressing fingers of sleep carrying me on an endless river, drifting and bobbing. And it happened again, at least twice, and my ribs banged and a lump on my head and the sudden loss of consciousness making me paranoid. I was at the law of diminishing returns, when alcohol no longer did what it was supposed to do. The sudden creepy and tightening corner I had steered my life to. The vacant feeling of meaninglessness.

What about my daughter, Rosalinda? And Monte, too? There was the sense of caring, the band of blood, the locked concept that we were of the same mother and father. I was upset, maudlin tears running down my cheeks. One more big glassful of vodka with a bare sprinkle of soda to disguise the medicinal taste. I could not stop the tears. Our Lady of Guadalupe. My hands shook violently, the taste of blood in my throat. Then blackness.

11 *Everyman's Business Agent*

When Monte came home he looked in the refrigerator. There was nothing solid to eat. He moved the jars of relish, the butter and milk aside and checked the freezer compartment. No loose steaks or even sandwich meat. While he was wondering what to eat, Pamela came into the kitchen. She was in a dressing robe but had makeup on, her gray hair brushed back neatly into a pageboy, and her fingernails a subdued red.

"There's nothing on the stove," Monte said. "What's for supper?"

"I never know when you're coming home," Pamela said. She adjusted her stockings so the seams were perfectly straight. "I wasn't able to buy anything today. You understand, if you take away the checkbook . . ."

Monte knew. She didn't want to argue, to bring up his taking her credit cards the previous week and deliberately cutting them up. She stood there adjusting her stockings, her suntanned face and the way she held her shoulders upright and the prematurely gray hair. He hardly remembered her hair not being gray. The fine features and the long bony hands—what he called the Connecticut horsewoman's hands. She had had a horse and still rode every day. Horses. Jesus Christ, if she had been a man, it would have been a string of polo ponies. As it was they belonged to the Sausalito Yacht Club. While he was working cargo, he must have been the only holdman on the West Coast with memberships in a yacht club and the symphony.

God, where did all the credit cards come from—the BankAmericard and Master Charge and Sears and Macy's and I. Magnin and Joseph Magnin, the Hertz card and American Express? He had been stroking cargo, nails in the hold, long beams of steel, and fish meal. The part-time stint as a shoveler, shoveling bones, and the copra docks and the whiskey ships at Pier Nine, and the grain docks and working sugar in Crockett and even napalm in

Redwood City, while she drifted through a world of perfume and operas and designer clothes. Five raincoats, all British and French, and thirty-eight pairs of shoes; he had counted them. She bruised and battered an inexhaustible supply of credit cards while he bruised and exhausted his body. How many times had he said, Enough, then reneged on his demands as she wheedled and used her series of tricks—shutting off all the goodies, complaints to their parish priest that he had taken the checkbook away from her. How many times had he collected the credit cards and neglected to pick up one and had her run that one into the ground? Darrell, their son, going to Brown University. Her idea, Monte recalled. He voted for USC or UCLA or USF. They were expensive enough without traveling to an eastern school.

But it was a losing game. When Darrell was still in kindergarten, Pamela bought him a bathing suit, a little boy's bathing suit. Monte recalled the details, that the lady at the counter had asked, "Cash or charge?" With those bright gray cats' eyes, Pamela intimated that she didn't have a credit card and never one at that particular store, neglecting to tell the saleslady that her husband had already placed a moratorium on all credit cards. The saleslady had the form out, and Pamela put her best cultured scrawl on it. Then she went through a couple of hundred dollars for a canvas beach chair and a complete collection of kid's sand toys, rubber ducks, brightly colored pails, small matching sand shovels, and a teeny weeny life preserver for her little dream boy. Mother's little boy. God, that woman is wearing me out, Monte told himself. Her life stretched as far as the cord on her hair dryer.

"Do you have any money?" she asked. Tomorrow was payday, but she knew he carried a small bankroll at all times. Monte peeled off a twenty, and Pamela disappeared into the bedroom. He carefully poured a couple of ounces of VO over one cube of ice and added a splash of soda. He sat looking at the glass, ruminating. Even the drinking glasses were fancy, fine crystal. Did she think he was Daddy Warbucks? God, how long does it take to get dressed? He poured another drink and loosened his tie, carefully hung his suit coat in the closet. For one second he fingered three or four of his Brioni suits, being careful not to match or compare his tastes with hers.

She was taking a long time to get ready. Maybe she wanted the butcher shop to close so she could pick up some ready-made food at the gourmet shop. Monte was working on his third drink when she came out of the bedroom, wearing the black blouse and tan woolen suit, the matching purse and gloves, the small earrings he had given her in Mexico City. Monte didn't belabor her time in getting dressed, only it seemed unusually long for someone just going to the store for some meat, maybe fresh vegetables, and a dessert. Give the devil her due. She could throw a meal together at a minute's notice and was never upset when he came home with company. A party was a party. How she enjoyed a party, accepting the compliments about how she dressed and the cleanliness of the house.

Monte poured a fourth drink while waiting for her to return, shaking his head from side to side as he weighed her good side against her bad. Her manners were above par, always courteous to both men and women. Her volunteer work uptown and for the parish helped his name and, he was smart enough to know, helped him politically.

An hour went by, then another half hour. Where the hell is that woman? Monte asked himself. He poured another drink, a little light on the VO.

Bad enough to have one alki in the family. Would Joe never learn? The merry-go-round goes round and round. How many times had he been to jail? The time he went to Pleasanton to bail Joe out for drunk and disorderly and found Zack in the same cell. Both of them talking racing-form talk all the way back—how they always had the first or the second horse of the exacta but never both. How the trainer had held back the favorite. How grey horses were never front-runners and the time of the feature race . . . 1.09 flat. A couple of drunken horseplayers and longshoremen —but one of them was his brother. The dryout tanks. The hospitals. The detox centers, medical and nonmedical. Monte decided it would have been better if he was a doctor or a lawyer. That's what Joe needed for a brother—not some business agent, who had a bad back like the rest of the longshoremen and a few broken bones and sawdust in his head. Joe and his crowd were loyal supporters, and they'd better be. They were always in trouble, and Monte the savior had to hustle and explain and downright lie to get them off the hook.

Goddamn American women will drive us looney. Monte recalled Joe's ex-wife, Maria Teresa, and wondered whatever happened to the girl. Rosalinda had been a replica of her mother. She had none of the Karsten features. Leggy like her mother. Joe's wife had a nonstop shape plus a little schoolhouse upstairs. She didn't go to school just to eat her lunch as Pamela had, Monte conceded.

Marriages were hard to figure. On the Las Vegas betting line, Joe and Maria Teresa's would be the favorite. The blistering love Joe had for his wife, and booze was not a problem then. The way Joe rode his daughter proudly on his shoulders. The shy, reticent Latina wife, the Portuguese style of good cooking, and the church as the center of the house. He and Pamela used the church as a social club, but to Maria Teresa it was a soul attachment. The scapulars on the wall, the crucifix in the bedroom, her style of having every room, even an apartment no matter how small, blessed by the priest. Her faith in God and Saint Martin of Porres, solidified by Joe's faith in her. And it all went wrong.

But he and Pamela were still together. Why was he still with Pamela? Maybe habit. He really didn't know. Why did Joe drink as if he wanted to destroy himself? By now Monte had taken off his narrow, black, polished Bally shoes, so soft to his feet. A man had to protect his feet, he thought. He nursed his drink. If he took another he might be sorry for what he would say.

Two and a half hours from the time she left, Pamela came through the door, not a single package in her hands. No shopping bag. Nothing.

"Where the hell have you been?" he asked.

"Monte," her voice dragged out. He knew she had had a few drinks. "Oh Monte, you must try the bouillabaisse at Pierre's, the new place down the block on Union. It's only been open for a month, and it was packed. For twelve-ninety-five, the bouillabaisse is superb. Super!" She emphasized the last word as if she was about to kick her leg high in the air, 1920s style.

Monte's eyes picked up all of her expressions. If he had had a gun in his hands, he would have drilled her right between the eyes. One small, neat black hole in her forehead, right between her eyes.

"Did you take that twenty and go down to a fancy creepy French joint and buy an overpriced bowl of soup for yourself knowing, knowing . . . ?"

His voice became more subdued, as if he was talking to a small child. All day long he dealt with children. The longshoremen were not some powerful, violent, revolutionary group of men. They were spoiled little kids, banging their high chairs with their little oatmeal spoons—spoiled little kiddies who wanted all the goodies but didn't want to go to the union meetings or to the Stewards Council. They were children who didn't understand the hard-driving price. Pamela was another spoiled brat.

He shifted to another gear. It was exasperating, but it wasn't the end of the world. He was a victim of rationality, had the ability to see two sides. Still it was disconcerting. She was not to be trusted to go out for a simple shopping excursion without fucking up. "Two hours. Did they have to import the soup from France?"

"The owner bought me a drink, and I told him about you. The piano player bought me a drink. Mind you, I didn't have a seat and didn't order right away. We sang two songs, and I'm under orders to be sure to bring you with me the next time . . . Monte, don't cross your eyes when I'm talking to you. Take that smile off your face. It's not even funny. The butcher's was closed and . . ."

"And what?" Monte shrugged. He had a fistful of twenties and fifties in his pocket. Tired as he was, he began to put on his shoes. "Leave your jacket on," he said. "We can go downtown. I'll have a snack. Maybe we can have a few dances at the Starlight Room." Why make it a total loss? Monte asked himself.

When they came back from dancing, Monte helped Pamela off with her coat. He knew her moods. If he wanted a little dancing in bed, he had to keep her laughing and in an upbeat mood. Pamela was tipsy and playful, but he had been through this American dream before. Taking her to a fancy bar in Mexico City—after a few drinks, having her hands caress his neck. And if he captured the exact moment and they took a cab back to the hotel and ran up the stairs—or better yet caught an elevator—and the Mexican Light and Power Company didn't run out of electricity and the elevator arrived at their floor and they hurried into the room caressing and stroking, then maybe he'd get a piece of ass. But if anything—any disruptive event, too much drinking on Pamela's part or the mention of her spending sprees or any arguments about credit or credit cards—came up, then kiss sex goodby. He had married Juliet and ended up with Lady Macbeth.

What a fucking helluva way to live, Monte thought. Pamela had never been hot and was now colder still, an iceberg in love with her own sickness: spending money. I'm wearing myself out trying to thaw this monumental cake of ice, Monte decided. But he still tried. He sweet talked Pamela, put soft music on the stereo, turned off the lights and lit a candle, ran to the kitchen to mix two more drinks, thought he heard her singing in the bathroom. He sat on the couch still as a mouse, waiting for Pamela and nursing a vision of her in a sheer negligee. The horseback riding and swimming kept up her shape. Monte drinking and waiting. Finally he went to the bedroom, half expecting her to pull him in with her. She was snoring and he shook her and she said, "What?"

"Are you going to sleep?" Monte asked.

"Yes. I'm tired . . . Monte don't bother me. We've been through this so many times."

"Are you sleeping with someone during the day?"

"No, no, no . . . that's all you have in your head."

"No, that's not all I have in my head. If I did, I'd have someone stake you out and find out for sure."

"Monte, what you have in your head is sex, sex, sex. And dear, tomorrow . . . sugar . . . I want to sleep now. Please?"

Monte tried to climb into bed with her and grab her breast. She twisted, and as he moved his hands, she locked her legs tight as a vise. She held her face pressed to the pillow so he couldn't kiss her. "I said tomorrow. Monte, now you're making me mad."

Monte began to feel silly. This was like school kids in the back of a car at some drive-in movie.

"Besides, I have a headache. Dearest, I really do. Monte, don't do that or we won't even get together tomorrow."

Monte was embarrassed, not because of Pamela, but for his own behavior. He gave her a dry kiss, turned off the light at the night-stand, went to the front room, and plunked himself down on the couch. She was no more than an expensive doll, a hollow dummy inside. He was fed up, but he couldn't afford to leave her. Too many things were in the hopper now. He knew he couldn't exhaust his energies fighting in a courtroom over a woman and the kid and the money and the house. He had lived in Cow Hollow around Union Street in this part of the Marina for years. He knew everyone and did not want to move.

But most important, this was election time, and he knew if he played his cards right he might have a good chance for the presidency of the local. He had waited for this supreme stepping-stone, and all systems said go. He was within reach, not that a divorce or separation would knock out his chances. The longshoremen understood human frailty. Even murder or being a dope addict might not keep him from the president's chair, but why take a chance? Pamela would never leave. But there were other ways to skin a cat. Eddie Tijera, his protector or goon, had a moonlighting job tending his brother's bar. The bar was full of hookers and topless-bottomless dancers, and Eddie was a super fixer-upper. All he had to do was call Eddie, and he'd have some slim little twist, some foxy gal with a stunning shape and a retarded mind. Monte knew over the long haul that he could not handle that.

What do you do when life doesn't go the way you want it to go? He had wound Pamela up like a toy, and the toy should have gone in a certain direction. But it didn't. Toys seldom did. The sign of maturity was to recognize one fact—that you don't always get your own way. But Monte always had a game plan, and over the years it worked, though sometimes slower than expected. The moon wasn't going to fall from the sky because he wined and dined his wife and she wouldn't come across.

Monte dreamed his dreams. He went into the kitchen and made another drink, then brought ice and soda and the bottle of VO back into the front room. He heard a foghorn in the distance, sometimes the screech of a car as it turned the corner. The city was asleep, only the night workers pumping the slow pulse of the city, waiting for the day to break. He remembered the latest convention in Honolulu. He had been fixed up. She was Chinese and thin as a saber, under orders to give him a good time . . . in the evenings at the beach at Waikiki. And the one afternoon that he got away, they flew to the rain forest on the Big Island. He had her on the soft grass with mist falling and goofy little birds hopping about. He came twice. That was a high-water mark for these last few years. Her name was Lola Lee. Wait for me, Lola Lee.

And at the nightclub, when Eddie took over for his brother. A slick cutesy blonde all over, new to the topless-bottomless routine. Monte had taken her in the back room on a desk. Her little squeaks and squeals—you'd have thought she was Marilyn Monroe.

Later, standing outside the bar, watching all the action on O'Farrell. The bulky transvestite, with arms bigger than a weight lifter's, swishing across the street. Eddie hinted that the motherfucker should be working cargo. And the hippies, the one girl with writing on her T-shirt—"I fuck for men who avoid the draft." Monte was curious and observant, but this was not his kind of action. Men with mustaches in evening gowns and men with jewelry and beads. Girls wearing old-fashioned clothes, older than his mother's time. These kids sleeping on park benches and driving by in old hearses with tubas and violas sticking out the back. The time he stopped for a light by the Panhandle near Haight Street. A youngster in a goofy old-fashioned dress came up to his car and said, "Suck your cock for ten bucks, mister?" He asked her, "How old are you?" She said, "Old enough." "Why don't you go back to Nebraska or Iowa or wherever you came from?" She said, "Fuck you in the ass, you old creep."

The city had changed since the Vietnam trouble began. For the first time in his life Monte looked at himself as an old man or at least middle aged. What is middle aged? Someone ten years older than yourself. The time he had gone over to the Ali Baba with Walter the gang boss. After waltzing around the dance floor for two hours, they picked up two women and took them out for a late-night breakfast. The women talked about their grandchildren, and the one he was with had false teeth. The entire night was a fiasco, the action at the dance too slow for him. He told Walter, "I'm looking for a piece of ass but not with a menopausal widow."

Monte poured another drink, but he drank so slowly that he never lost consciousness. A faint light was coming through the curtains, garbagemen clanking their cans. He began to doze off. The night was dissolving into a high-tree jungle, the city melting down like chocolate. The cats are out, he cautioned himself. The clunky toot of the ferryboats for Sausalito. The cabs lingering in front of the Saint Francis, hoping for trips to the airport. Palmtree Jack sleeping under the trees in Union Square. The buses clanking through Chinatown. All the working stiffs taking their coffee royals before they caught buses for work. Soon Montgomery Street would have the lovely and long-legged gals heading for their jobs at the brokerage houses. Stock prices already known on the East Coast, ready to be transferred to the West. The entire West

Coast waiting for the early glow of the sun. The *Oriana* due today, the big British ocean liner coming in from Honolulu and Hong Kong and Singapore. The smells of coffee and pepper and cinnamon and tea from the docks. The pelicans and seagulls and cormorants dipping their beaks into the bay for fish. The early morning swampers, cleaning Fisherman's Wharf before the run of tourists. The rats and mice scurrying for their holes at the alien stomp of human feet. Finally, the big glow of sun from over the Sierras. . . .

Zing, zing, zinging. Monte straightened up, quickly took in his surroundings. He grabbed the ringing phone. It was Carney, a holdman in Walter's gang, and a fuckup.

"Where are you?" Monte asked. "San Jose! You were in a chimney, and the morning swamper found you? What fireman? They had to use a hook and ladder? What's the charge?"

Monte listened to the voice of Carney, five-thirty in the morning, appealing, "Monte, they're trying to book me for breaking and entering. Burglary and robbery. Monte, are you coming down to court today? Are you?"

"Yes, I'm coming down. I'll have the bail, if there is bail. I want to know one thing, Carney. How the fuck did you ever get caught in a chimney?"

"Monte, don't get mad. I can explain. I was stuck halfway down and couldn't scramble up or slide down. Are you coming?"

"Yes, yes, I'm coming. Like Jesus, I'm coming. If I don't make the hearing, plead not guilty."

"Bring a lawyer."

"Don't worry about a lawyer," Monte said. "I'll worry about that. Just dummy up. Don't make any deals. Where was it?"

"The Black Angus Restaurant. Don't laugh, Monte. I'm in some trouble."

"Don't talk to anyone until I get there." Monte hung up. He took the ice dish, the bottle of soda, and the half-bottle of VO into the kitchen. He put on a percolator of coffee, making it stronger than usual. He sat in the kitchen waiting for the coffee to perk. With the first whiff of coffee and the taste just right, he took out a cigar and lit it. Only three deep draws, then he put the cigar in an ashtray. The sun was up. Another day, and Monte was beginning to run.

III *The Detox Center*

Monte put me in the Valencia detox. He must have; I was in no condition to do it myself. Booze had driven me to hospitals and detox centers many times before, but I was never in Valencia. I knew the building, a large Victorian in the sunny part of San Francisco.

Nighttime, and the lights of the cars crisscrossing the ceiling. No matter how I turned in bed, there was no comfortable position. When I sat up, I began to tremble. My body exploded with sweat, and I felt so faint that I was on the verge of passing out. Whenever I lay back, all the garbage of my life swirled through my head. All the cars I had banged up. Burning rubber and wrecked cars. Sawdust old ladies spilled out on freeways. Red lights I had run. Always forgetting where I had parked the car. Driving home in a blackout, through a plate glass of some florist shop or through the doorway of a police station. Casing out the bumper, never knowing if I had demolished some kids in a crosswalk. Fumbling fingers rattling the newspaper, heart thumping as I searched for an article about a hit and run. My checking account a shambles. The checks I had kited to cover the other checks.

When I closed my eyes, the scenes shuffled through, movielike. Fear that at my age I would end up in a penitentiary with all the low riders and Blacks and Mexicans, forced to choose sides. For a second the entire set of scenes subsided, and there was just a flash window open to reality. Would I, a Navy veteran and a functioning citizen of San Francisco, be fingerprinted and cashiered to some penitentiary for a few accidents and a few measly bad checks? The scenes and the self-imposed horror shifted so rapidly that I could not resolve or conjecture or decide. My entire existence was placed within these shifting scenes of action and inaction and distress and the sick, paranoid feeling that I was alone and the entire outside world was after me.

There was no way to tell time. No watches, only calculations as a result of the amount of traffic on the street outside or the appearance of the sun, which never seemed to come. Traffic subsided, and then a long unending silence. A vision of breakfast and the zombie shuffling of feet in the pale green corridor. No. Night crashed my hopes. The night had stretched, the silence grew longer and longer, the scenes more deadly. Cemeteries and ghostly hands reaching out of the graves. Brutal accidents on the waterfront and the steady dismantling of bodies, screams in the night.

All the aches and pains, the fibrillations of my heart. The sharp-needle pain in my liver and kidneys, the gagging dashes to the toilet down the hall, the weak sweat-ridden staggers back to bed. Covers over my head, gurgles and groans of the others sleeping in the long room with me. Occasionally, the pinpoint of a cigarette a few beds away.

The first night in detox was a night without sleep. A constant shifting in bed, readjusting the covers, watching the ceiling and listening. Listening for what? Waiting for the counselor's flashlight? The entire pattern repeated over and over. The sweat-stained guilt payoff for all the sins of my life, imagined or true.

Morning. The entire detox center was much more pleasant and safer bathed in light. I couldn't eat, but I shook my way through sips of orange juice and Sanka. I craved cold milk, but I could not hold the glass. I tried a paper cup but spilled milk in both attempts to get it to my mouth. Food was plentiful and available at all hours, even after meals . . . cookies, chocolate, fruit, and ice cream.

This is nonmedical detox. Meaningless words to an outsider— nonmedical detox. To people on the circuit, it has an ominous meaning. No pills, no shortcuts to eliminating the horrors and the shakes. The good food and the congenial surroundings don't shortcut the trembles and the dribbles and the vomiting and the hallucinations and the convulsions. There is no Librium, no Valium, not even one stinking aspirin. Tough it out, buster. Tough it out, you sick and stupid dog. Sympathy is a word between shit and chancres. Valencia detox, a cold, heartless place of cheap smiles and no pills, no condolences and little empathy. A place to be avoided. Why had Monte shoved me in here?

I had been here two days. Monte came by. The cheerful bullshit smile. The "How're you doing, you're looking good" therapy way he has of talking. The expensive Italian suit. The shirts that are so original and up-to-snuff, modern. He is swift-talking. In some lights he reminds me of a carnival barker, in others, an old-fashioned matinee idol. But I know better than to underestimate Monte. The other side of the coin is that Monte is a shrewd, practical, realistic survivor. He is the best business agent Local 10, the longshoremen, have had. A man who will get up at three in the morning to help a union member in distress, visit hospitals, search out lawyers or shrinks. He's a friend of any union member who can vote. No story is too out of line for Monte to appreciate. "I can get you out of any place but the cemetery" is his motto. And he's even moved dead union members from Holy Cross to Wood-lawn at a wife's or mother's request. He is everyone's homegrown lawyer, everyone's homegrown psychiatrist. But you have to be a voting union member in good standing. Oh, Monte has taken the shirt off his back and has given it to bums on the piers, and he has thrown money away in bars and on loans to families and to long-shoremen and to derelicts. But that's an exaggeration of his style. He chops and clips everything and everyone down to his size.
He is a free-swinging big spender and a strong vote-getter. Memory of an elephant. A fast, mask-changing son of a bitch. Don't cross him. Don't cross him. He can be cold as ice. Monte is an old-time guy with a modern style. I'm his brother, and I can't fathom all the masks.

"How come you brought me in here?"

Monte had his fedora in his lap. For a second he fingered his tie. "Couldn't get you into anyplace else. I tried the Marine Hospital. I know it's a country club, and you could come down much easier with the doctors and all that medico bullshit. But it's only one time around for anyone who is not a seaman or an Indian or a coast-guardsman. I had a tough time getting you in there the last time; I had to kiss ass. Would you rather go up to Duffy's in Calistoga and listen to his Marine Corps bullshit or to the Howard detox with all the real sick winos? This place has a few stockbrokers and some nice gals."

"Nice gals?"

"Well, no Playboy bunnies, but you're in no condition to handle them anyway. Joe, I got you into the best place I could on short notice. Better than the indian detox at Laguna. Remember when you were there with twenty-six indians? Hey, things are not so bad."

Monte slipped me a ten-dollar bill. He zipped open the airline bag beside his polished shoes just enough for me to peer in. "Some cigarettes, cigars, and candy, clean shorts and shaving gear. I know how rough their company razors are, especially with the shakes. Do you need an electric razor? I have an extra. Okay, I'll bring it next time. Call me any time. Sweetdick and Borrego said to say hello. Pamela also. Incidentally, you have a friend upstairs. He's banging his head against the walls. I just brought him in."

"Who?" I asked.

"Why don't you let it be a surprise. He's one of your gang. One of your old-time drinking buddies. Good luck and take care of yourself."

We shook hands. I slumped into the chair. I heard Monte on the way out, talking to the counselors. The high laugh of the woman we called the Warden. I had never heard her laugh before . . . Monte was the original one man band.

When I went up to the men's ward, the one with the twelve beds, there was Siberia Sam, his head thrown back without a pillow and flat on his back. No movement, still as a dead man except for involuntary twitches. I hadn't expected Siberia Sam. Sam was an alki, but I had never seen him in detox before. He was another example of Monte's good works. I had expected Roger, who had been in so many dryout farms and detox centers that he'd qualify as a guide.

Siberia Sam. An old-time seaman. A communist party member who had carried the banner for years. He had a Marxian clamp on his head, a card-carrying lefty. But he was more than that. His big regret was that he had been too young to fight in the Spanish Civil War.

Booze cuts everyone down to size. Siberia Sam was proof. He should have been home making bombs in the basement or typing up proclamations. Instead, he was flat on his back, dead drunk, immobilized, a victim of John Barleycorn. I padded back to my armchair in the living room.

Sam had two convulsions in the next two hours. I held down his feet. This was the modus operandi at the detox. Everyone helped. The idea was that this was a social setting and the setting was part of the cure. Each resident—they were careful not to call us patients —helped to calm and influence other residents. But if withdrawal became too chaotic or nerve-wracking, they sent the troublemaker to a hospital. Some of the drunks faked heart attacks just to get to the Librium or Valium. Shaking it out cold turkey is no fun.

Siberia Sam's convulsions disoriented him. By early evening they decided to ship him to Presbyterian, the big hospital over the hill, not too far from where I lived. The short, snotty woman we called the Warden came over to my chair.

"Do you know that man? Sam Suslenoff?"

"Yes, I know him. Siberia Sam. He's a longshoreman, just like me."

"Go up and keep him company. We're making arrangements to send him to the hospital."

"Why not leave him here? We can help him 'melt down' and come out of it."

"He's had four convulsions in as many hours."

"I thought he only had two."

"The last two were small, but he's hallucinating right now. I'd appreciate it if you'd try to keep him calm, at least until we get his papers ready."

Yes sergeant, yes chief. I'm jumping up and shaping up, Warden.

I went to see Siberia Sam. He was holding onto the bed covers, sitting straight up with his back against the bedboard, his shock of hair straight up. A week's growth of beard. A wild look in his eyes.

"What's up, Sam?" As I talked to him, I tried to get the covers from his grasp, but he kept chewing them. "Hey, old buddy, what's the big deal. We gotta get you out of them pajamas, into street clothes."

Sam making noises, animal noises, nothing distinguishable, his eyes constantly shifting toward the closet. I went over and peered in. A bunch of junky suitcases and Safeway shopping bags, with clothing piled in and on the suitcases and bags. Sam started to point. I tried to get him to his feet to guide him to the closet.

I didn't know what he wanted. Did he want clothes for the trip to the hospital; did he know he was going to the hospital? When I tried to help him up and direct him to the closet, he resisted.

"What do you want?" I asked.

More noises as if he was groaning. Then he began to mumble, at the same time pointing to the closet again. I opened the door wide so he could see inside.

"What?"

"He's in there."

"Who is?"

"Trotsky, and he has an axe."

"No one's in there, Sam. And why Trotsky? He's dead. And why does he need an axe for you? Maybe he wants to talk to you."

Sam drew his knees tight to his chest. "I don't want to talk to him."

"Why don't we go down and call Monte," I said. "That's Monte's game. He knows how to get rid of guys who hang around closets and try to chop up old friends." Joke him out of it. "Sam, maybe you better switch from vodka to gin. Then you'd have Churchill in the closet, and he's a good guy." But Sam had no interest in jokes. He was sad looking and sick. His sickness came out of the bottle, not from politics or theory.

Then Sam went into another convulsion and shit in his pants. We struggled to hold him down. An ex-con from Arkansas helped. We all took turns calming him until the Warden came. He was a mess to clean up.

Then Sam was on his way to a place where they had needles to calm a person down. I was glad that he was gone. In a way, as a union brother Sam was my responsibility. But I wasn't in shape to handle my own responsibility, much less his. He'd be in good hands. Besides, Monte would make sure he had top service.

The ex-con from Arkansas was one big bullshitter. I couldn't stand his type. It wasn't that he's an ex-con. The waterfront has a few guys who came out of the joint. We pay no attention to them. Some are easy guys, and some are trouble. Can't be trusted. Arkie didn't make me wary, not that kind of danger. He wasn't a hype, and I doubted if he packed a gun. But in his own way he was a slimy son of a bitch. He ferreted me out, never giving me a chance to stay put, relax in the chair, and nod to that sentimental and dreamy forties and fifties music. The music that makes you think the world is sweet and charming—no bum checks or police cars staked out outside your hotel. No rats in the hallways or cockroaches climbing the walls. When you listen to KABL or KFOG, no assassins linger in the closets. No axe wielders, not even old daddy-o Trotsky himself. All closet doors are closed, and there is a moratorium on all hallucinations and convulsions. The woman is in a summery dress and a picture hat, as I paddle the canoe around the lake in Golden Gate Park. Ex-con Arkie didn't leave me alone. "You're the only hep guy around here." That was his opening line.

I noted that he has conned me out of two packs of cigarettes since the night before.

"I want to finish that story," he said.

"We don't have enough time."

"We've got nothing but time. Remember, I told you the first time I went in I had this love affair where I was the girl. Then the second time, I had this terrific little fish, blond hair and an ass that wouldn't quit—would not quit."

In a ghoulish way he got me interested, because I know very little about his kind of life.

"This year's love affair becomes next year's competition," I said.

"Were you ever in the joint?"

"Never," I said. "I'm just guessing."

"That's the way it goes."

"I don't want to talk about jails and joints, people being cooped up. I'm cooped up in here, and that's enough. What have you done since you got out?"

I already knew he didn't work. He was on SSI or was riding one of those state or federal agencies that keeps sickos from working or tries to readjust ex-cons.

He kept leaning closer to me so the others couldn't hear. "I go to Saint Anthony's kitchen where everyone is lined up in the morning waiting for a meal. I usually carry a half-gallon of wine in a paper bag. I stand in line and approach some bum. This has worked every time. I've never missed. I say, 'After we chow up, do you want to come up to my room and drink up a storm?' I hint that I have another bottle in the room. Sometimes we go up without eating, because he needs wine more than food. We go up and drink, then go to bed."

"Go to bed and what?"

"We fuck. We have a relationship."

"You and some crummy bum?"

"Yes."

"Does he take a bath?"

"Sometimes."

"And you blow him or he blows you?"

"Whatever. Sometimes we fuck each other in the ass."

"Why don't you go to work?"

"What's that got to do with this?" He shook his head as if I was some dope who didn't understand, didn't know the meaning of nirvana. "I'm on assistance. I get three hundred and eighty-six bucks a month and that's enough. I eat at Saint Anthony's and try to score with some wino, maybe once or twice a week."

"And you're satisfied with that kind of life. Come out of a penitentiary, sit on your ass with some government funding, eat free at a mission, and stick your dick up some old wino's ass. You call that living?"

"And you think you're living, working six days a week to support some woman who won't even give you a piece of ass most of the time? Paying off her bills and living in some joke of a house?"

I reached over and took his cigarettes. They were really mine. I pushed them into my pocket. "Get your fucking ass away from me. You're not even a degenerate. You're a fucking sick freeloading motherfucker, and I hope some wino erases your throat some night. Not with his cock but a cold steel blade. That will save me tax money if nothing else. Fuck off." I helped him with a shove.

After supper most of the TV watchers went into the other room. We had a couple of women comedians, but they were released late that afternoon. Arkie the ex-con made a wide detour around me. We had a visitor, a former alumnus of the place. He walked through and passed out cigarettes. The soft-touch radio played "Please Release Me" and part of the score from *My Fair Lady*. I made a new friend. He was a teamster who went by his last name, Sackville. Very British, though he was some sort of Eastern European. I told him my story, how many days I had been drinking, how many days without food before Monte dragged me in here. I went over the reasons why I hadn't taken a shower or a bath in two weeks. He kept nodding his head. When I finished, he said, "That doesn't make you a bad guy."

His story. He had a girlfriend, and it was evident he had someone taking care of the essentials. His shoes were shined, his shirts and pajamas ironed, plenty of smokes, all the paraphernalia for shaving, and toothbrushes, tweezers, scissors, clippers. Most residents come in barren and broke. Sackville was sick enough and bewildered, but he hadn't hit bottom. A high-bottom drunk.

"I'd been drinking for a few weeks straight, not working. Somehow I ended up downtown—hiking up Powell Street with a shaggy lion chewing on my arms and legs and me fighting him off. The people on the cable car watching, the lion growling, and me screaming and yelling."

"Where did the lion come from?" I asked. "What kind of lion, anyway?"

"An African lion, a stupid shaggy lion. Maybe he escaped from a zoo. Maybe he was born here or came over on a ship and walked down the gangplank like a visitor. He wasn't bothering anyone else," Sackville said convincingly. "I couldn't get rid of him. They're a hazard, you know. I remembered a doctor I'd had some dealings with. He was in a medical building on Sutter Street. I proceeded up Powell with the cable car clanging and this stupid lion hanging on by his teeth with me dragging him uphill. The doctor said there was an easy way to get rid of the lion. Quit drinking. I told him I didn't want to get rid of the lion that much. He wasn't a pushy doctor. He told me the lion was a hallucination and that hallucinations are not necessarily bad. That I should make friends with my hallucination."

Sackville and I were sitting up through the night, smoking up a storm. I had finished seven cigars and was working on my third pack of cigarettes—Pall Malls, which is not my brand.

"Where is the lion now?" I asked.

"He's here with us. Sitting right there. I had to sneak him in. The Warden doesn't like any kind of pet. But he's really not a pet. He's a goddam pest. One consolation, he's eating all the mice. I have a bowl of milk for him. Most important, I don't want him following me wherever I go. I'm entitled to some privacy."

With that Sackville stood up and kicked the lion, not once but three or four times. And since I was part of the gag and also sharing Sackville's cigarettes, I got up and kicked the lion a few times.

"Does he disturb your girlfriend?" I asked.

"No, not really," Sackville's tone became low and serious as if she might be listening. "She doesn't believe there is a lion. She thinks I'm a cuckoo and should be up in Mendocino to get my head straight instead of drinking and coming in and out of detox places like a yo-yo. Do you believe there is a lion, Joe?"

"There are two ways of looking at it. In one way, and probably her way, there is no lion. But in our way there might be. He's sort of a symbol. In order to get rid of him, you have to get rid of a certain way of living. Let's say he's an imaginary lion who at this particular time is here. Yes, actually here. But if we change our way of living and quit drinking, he might slink away."

"You're smart for a longshoreman," Sackville said.

"Smart enough to be in here," I said.

Arkie's gone. Sackville's gone. Siberia Sam was over at Presbyterian being cooled off with drugs. The counselors wanted me to leave and go into some program—Garden Sullivan, where they have an encounter group or Laguna Honda, where they have a twenty-eight-day program with exercise and yoga or Alcoholics Anonymous, God forbid or the ninety-day program down the Peninsula. I kept stalling. If I don't take a program, eventually they'll just dump me out in the street. I just wanted to get my head straight, go back home, and go to work. Meanwhile I sat in the armchair listening to the songs from KFOG—"Lara's Theme" from *Doctor Zhivago*, and "Spanish Eyes" and "Maria Elena." The Warden said that if I listen to this music long enough, I'll never be able to have children.

A woman started to sleep on the couch across from me. Her name was Sandy. She was a loner—didn't have much to do with the other women in detox. She lay with her back toward me, hardly ever on her back looking at the ceiling. Sometimes there were evil things on the ceiling. Not talkative or communicative.

But often she checked to see if I was still sitting across from her. She had short blonde hair and good features, though her nose might be too long. Couldn't tell about her shape, never saw her standing up. Besides, she was in those sack pajamas.

About two in the morning she stirred. "Does the radio disturb you?" I asked.

"No, nothing like that." As she talked, she tried to raise up but kept falling back.

"I'm gonna make some chocolate," I said. "Do you want any?"

"Is there any cold milk?"

"Sure."

I puttered around the kitchen and put on water for the chocolate. I brought her back a glass of milk and a handful of cookies. We did this for the rest of the night—milk, chocolate, orange juice, and not much talking. I told her my name and she told me hers. The next day after the morning cleanup, she moved to a chair next to me, a blanket wrapped around her body and legs. She had to move, as people were seated all over and it was hard for someone to lie full length on the couch during daytime.

"There's a small room upstairs for women," I said. "Why don't you go up there? It's more comfortable than the couch."

"I don't want to do that. Do I bother you or keep you awake at night?" she asked.

"No, not at all. I have a bed upstairs and my junk is in the closet. But I can't sleep. Whenever I lie flat out, all the garbage of my life swings around. I find it easier to sit up and smoke and listen to the radio. Nighttime is the only time I can relax. But I can't lie down and go to sleep."

"I won't bother you," she said.

"Why are you sleeping down here at night?"

"I told them a story about the beds and my back."

"But that's not it?"

"No. Can we keep this to ourselves? Otherwise they think I'm trying to stir up trouble. This is the third time I've been here. The last time I was sleeping up in the women's room, really zonked out, and didn't notice that I was up there alone. I woke up and some man was masturbating onto my face, coming just as I woke up."

"Did you scream?"

"No, I didn't even call the counselors. It was so dark that I couldn't pick up on his features or even his color. It was pitch black. I had a feeling about his size, and I could break it down to three or four guys in the detox but no closer than that. After that, I wouldn't even go down to the laundry room to wash my underwear."

"I don't want to sound grotesque, but how do you know I won't get up in the night and do the same thing to you?"

"There's a small lamp on all night, and I'd know it was you. But I asked a woman about you. She said you're a workingman, a longshoreman—and a straight guy. Not like the rest of these creeps."

"Yeah, I'm a straight guy, and I write my life out using a straight pencil but with a lot of crooked lines. We'll be friends."

I stuck out my hand. She cautiously reached one hand out from the blanket. I shook her fingers, which were trembling and icy cold.

In the afternoon I went down to wash my socks and a shirt. I asked if she wanted something washed.

"Come on, we're friends. Don't be embarrassed. This is not the place to be embarrassed." When I took her brassiere and her underpants, I shoved them into my shirt, then went down the stairs and threw them into the washer. The emphasis placed on women in *Vogue* magazine is not the same emphasis we place on them at Valencia.

We didn't need to ask questions, just confided personal information naturally. I told Sandy about the longshoremen and how my brother Monte shot up to the top in union politics, about our life when we were kids in Jackson, in the Gold Country. How our dad was lost in a mine disaster. How our mom moved to the city and raised us in Noe Valley, in the upper part of the Mission District only a few streets over from the detox. I told her that I was a baseball player when I was young and about being in the navy. How I'd always been a hunter and a fisherman and fishing in the surf on foggy mornings or up in the trout streams of Northern California. The steelhead runs. Standing in the cold river and the rain, as steelhead are a bad-weather fish, and that fishing for steelhead was better than having an orgasm with a knocked-out woman. How I quit all the outdoor stuff after I was divorced, unless one calls drinking bouts up in the Russian River outdoors. Lately, the trips to Reno boozing it up with the longshoremen. How I hung around the bars on Clement Street where I usually lived. That I also drank in the places along the waterfront. She asked if I had any children. I lied and said no.

My life seemed conservative alongside hers. It was evident she wanted to confide in someone. I guessed that she thought she would never see me again, unless it would be in some hospital or another detox. The chance of that was slim. People come and go in this booze action. The jails and penitentiaries and nut farms and psycho trips scatter them around. A person can't build a life on shifting sand.

"Are you lonesome or depressed?" I asked.

"I attempted suicide less than six months ago."

"I thought of it, but I never made a real attempt," I said. "It went through my mind to do it romantic. Go out in Frisco Jeans and a Hickory shirt from the top of the Golden Gate Bridge. But whenever I thought of it, my cars were wrecked. And I didn't have enough energy to walk to the top of the bridge." I lit a cigarette, watched her eyes for a second. They were hazel. "Where you from, anyway?"

"Los Angeles. My mom played an organ in church and directed the choir. She spent so much time in church she had no time left over for my sister and me. I loved my dad, but because mom neglected him so much he packed up and left. I was only seven years old at the time. From then on, I was raised haphazard."

I went to the kitchen and poured a glass of milk for her and made a cup of instant coffee for myself.

"I have nutty dreams sometimes, especially when I'm on a run," I said. "I have dudes in my dream telling my fortune, and it's always bad. Gold and red rats running over big maps. Monkeys playing pinochle on cable cars. And I guess as an insight to my fortune or future life . . . I'm on a gunboat going up a murky river. The flags flying from the stern, a flock of girl angels lining the rail, bands playing. The boat's going against the current and slowly going under at the same time. A few ripples and everything's over. No band, no angels, no boat, no flags, no me."

I lit another cigarette. "I haven't told anyone any of this stuff before. I don't think I ever told a woman, other than my wife, that my dad was lost in the mine. That his tomb is actually down below."

"Some people reveal more than others," she said. "I've been seeing a psychiatrist and he is zilch. He rarely talks. He's a real square, has a square head, square glasses, and his office is square. Every once in a while we come up with some clue, between us. Like that I'm out of touch with my own generation and really don't trust young people. I was hooked on heroin. In trying to kick heroin, I ended up an alcoholic. I must be a compulsive and addictive person. I originally used drugs from doctors' prescriptions to counter all my disabilities and ailments. I have epilepsy. Throughout my life I've had all kinds of operations, spinal taps, and brain scans. Whenever I'm screwed up and coming off junk, I'm a victim of grand mal seizures. Mom left me, psychologically, early in life. I've been on my own since I was sixteen. Sometimes I worked as a secretary. Joe, I even did a stint as a hooker, as a streetwalker on Sunset Boulevard."

"That's no big thing. Everybody's got to do something for a living. I can see that you might be a turn-on."

"Because of my unusual looks, I became a call girl in Beverly Hills. All this was for short periods, as I could never keep my life in focus. I wanted to be an artist, to paint or be a sculptor."

When women are in detox, you can never tell how they truly look. The sacky pajamas and the bruises on their bodies or faces, the ragdoll uncombed hair, pale faces with the dark circles under their eyes make them all look similar—that crazy, drifty look. When women ride the roller coaster down, they spend little time on makeup or hairdos.

I noticed that Sandy was tall, maybe five seven barefoot. She had started to comb her hair. It was short, blonde, and, as far as I could tell, natural. Slender body, slanty eyes. She claimed to have some Oriental blood mixed in with Danish and Swedish. But I paid no attention to that. For years on the waterfront and in the bars of the Tenderloin, every woman with pitch-black hair claimed she was part Cherokee. Currently it was fashionable in San Francisco to be Oriental. Sandy's features reminded me of a young but decadent movie star with a touch of the hippie.

"Did you ever marry?" I asked.

"No, though I've lived with a few men. The epilepsy made me leery of both marriage and sex. Living with a man gave me a sort of security. But I was never an explorer in the direction of sex. Some men thought me icy cold. The reason I opened up to you . . . Joe, I had an immediate receptivity to you. I get good vibes from you."

"I've been around people who are banged up for most of my life," I said. "The epilepsy doesn't bother me. If we were ever together and you had an attack, we could take care of it between ourselves. It's no big thing."

"When my life is in chaos, I have one attack right after another. Then other times I have them so seldom I think they've gone away. Now, I'm under sedation. No, not in here. I didn't say a word about epilepsy for fear I wouldn't get in. But when I'm under a doctor's or my psychiatrist's care, I take Dilantin and Valium. That seems to do the trick."

As she talked, in the afternoon light filtering in from the windows she was downright beautiful. The shakes had subsided, and as she emphasized words with her hands, I saw she had long fingers and well-kept nails. She had changed right before my eyes.

"I'm going to write down my address," I said. My phone is disconnected now, but I always have a phone. Take down the address. If you ever need a place to bed down or a meal. There are no women in my life, and you can stay as long as you want. I won't even make a pass at you." I'd been in detox before. All the exchanges of addresses and phone numbers meant little, because everyone went back to old vices and old friends and old haunts.

"Joe, I thought you said you lived in a hotel near the waterfront or in the Tenderloin."

"The last few days of my drinking run I was in a hotel. But I keep this place on Clement Street in the inner Richmond. I've had this small apartment for seven years. Whenever I'm on a drinking run my brother Monte pays the rent for me. Sometimes I forget where I live. Sometimes I forget the city. It's not odd for me to have keys to two or three hotel rooms at the same time. Just remember my home address, and if you lose the address, go to the 540 Club on Clement. If you're really desperate, check the Long-shoremen's Hall. The girls in the office won't give you my phone number or address, but they'll take a message. Tell me where I can get in touch with you, and I'll be around."

That night, when everyone else was asleep, she told me her true story, or so she said. She didn't have epilepsy but had appropriated —her word—the disease or affliction from her younger sister, who was the true victim. Her mother was never a churchgoer but was man crazy and lived with more than a dozen men while the girls were young—even married a few. Sandy emphasized that she did not know her true dad. She never used heroin, but it sounded romantic and gave her a good excuse for going down the drain. She was in L.A. and Hollywood only for a short time but was a call girl in Beverly Hills. She came from Wyoming, a small town near the Bighorn Mountains. When she was nine years old, she moved to Hayward with her mother and sister and another of her mother's husbands.

Vividly she remembered her first contact with sex. A man accosted her—or in a finer description, took her in with a little game. She was inside the schoolyard and didn't remember if it was recess or just after school. He coaxed her to play a game for some candy. She was not apprehensive, because she would stay on the inside of the picket fence and he would stay on the outside. The game entailed going along the fence together. They moved and he put his thumb through the fence. She would stroke his thumb. Then they moved to the next opening. In and out. But for the candy she had to close her eyes. The thumb seemed bigger. In truth, it grew with every stroke. She wasn't aware of the impact of the game, only the thumb growing bigger and bigger until he squirted all over her hand. He gave her the candy, waved as she backed away. After the scariness left her, she went back to the fence somewhere near the same time, but he never came back.

"And you never told anyone?"

"No, I kept it to myself. Maybe that's why the man jacking off in my face, the last time I was here, disturbed me so."

I didn't know what to say. First Siberia Sam. Then the degenerate ex-con. And I knew how to handle shaggy African lions, especially if they were not there. I've been around the block a few times. I don't shock easy. Most alcoholics are compulsive talkers when the shakes stop. But are they compulsive about the truth?

"I was tall for my age," Sandy said. "By the time I was fourteen I had gained my full height. Older men were attentive to me. I was forever sitting on older men's laps. Uncles and grandfathers, and a bunch of mixed-up and replaceable dads. They were always pawing me, and I had mixed feelings about that. It's hard to look back, but I guess I liked the attention."

"How did you ever start as a hooker?"

Sandy explained. When they lived in Hayward, her mother separated from a man who had been attentive to Sandy, a man who came close to treating her like a real daughter. One day walking home from school with her girlfriend, just after she had turned fourteen, she ran into this third or fourth husband of her mother's. They talked, and he gave her his address. He said that if she ever needed help to come by and see him, that he thought of her as a real daughter, and although he was separated from her mother, Sandy should think of him as a dad and even as a good friend.

It took her two weeks, but she went by. He asked if she had told her mother. She said she hadn't told anyone. He intimated that he was trying to help her. If she needed spending money or clothes, she was always welcome, that he would treat her. He'd appreciate it if she didn't tell her mom. She said not to worry, because she and her mom didn't get along. In truth, he knew they were competitive. He bought her clothes and gave her money, more than she expected.

She started going over once or twice a week. He was a slow mover, playing it safe. They began to kiss good-by. Then kisses after every gift. Then she started to model the clothes he bought for her. She understood his game as she teased him, one time modeling only in long blue stockings and gold Cuban heels. His fingers trembled as she allowed him to adjust the stockings. Then kissing her above the stocking on her upper thigh, and as she turned around, kissed her lovingly on her behind. "It was as big then as it is now," she confided to me.

Because of the kisses after every gift he began to buy gifts more often. They were expensive, and she had to keep them at his apartment so her mother wouldn't find out. One day they had wine for lunch and she smoked her first joint and felt woozy. He had her put on a white dress with long white stockings and the kind of garters that brides wear. She had on white high heels and nothing under the dress. He began kissing her legs, then her thighs, and then all over. By this time she was vibrating. He was much younger than her mother and by far her mother's best-looking husband. She succumbed, and he taught her to do the same for him.

He had a vivid imagination, and his imagination appealed to her. Occasionally, he had a friend who was much older come over. She had relations with the friend, and they passed her between them.

She acquired a small bank account. She also knew she had acquired control. They had control in that they had the money and the price for the fine perfumes and slick clothes. But she had the final control with her youth and her smooth body and her ability to shut off sex whenever she wanted. At that time and at her early age, she had not acquired a fear of men. She knew she was selling sex for money, and the sex pleased her.

She kept up this arrangement for two years, and then it ended. Her old-time daddy-lover was killed in a car accident. She saw the older man two more times, but he wanted her to dress in leather and control him more than she wanted to. She was tired of this game, and she cooled him.

Without finishing high school, Sandy went to San Francisco and disappeared into the mass of hippies who flooded the city. But she got tired of being dirty all the time. She liked to dress up more than the other girls, and she wanted a more structured life. I guess she learned the encounter and psychological words from her therapist. She wanted a job, and her own money, and an apartment without people piling in, sleeping all over the floor, and scrounging her food. She didn't like the dope and the pimps and the hustle, people hustling her all the time, abusing her. She condemned pimps most of all. She hated people who never took a bath. She liked the beginning of being a hippie, the freedom and wandering in the park, the flowers and sunshine. She was baffled by the trying-out of all kinds of drugs, the wild zombie effects, the colors running through her head. Sometimes she had the feeling of being in a small town in the West, a child's version of Wyoming. But the heavy dope and the violence and the pimps and all the nuts preying on the hippies made her leave that scene.

She moved downtown and worked as a waitress in a restaurant.

She used most of her tips to buy clothes, to help her get a job in fashion or some aspect of art.

Once, on her day off, she was doing her clothes in a launderette. She was wearing high heels and a dress, ready to look for a better job. A man came in and asked if she'd like a job in a massage parlor, that she could do it just for a day. He said that she didn't have to do anything she didn't want to do or go into a room with any man who turned her off. She needed the money, and she wanted to quit the waitress job with its long hours, poor pay, and low tips. So she tried the massage parlor for one day and made a lot of money. More than she ever had. She tried it for a week and extended it to three months. Then she decided that if she was to be a hooker—the massage was a hype—she had to eliminate the middleman. She picked up pointers from the others girls and took an apartment a few blocks from the massage parlor. Off and on for the next few years she had apartments in Berkeley and in San Francisco. For a short time she had a place in Beverly Hills. Near the end of her hooking days, she did a stint walking the streets on the western end of Sunset Boulevard.

"I liked it at first," Sandy said. "Then it got to be old hat. Nothing ever changed. I still had old men pawing over me, though some were nice and generous. I had to use Valium or Seconal to put me to sleep. Joe, one time I flew to Mexico City to buy a thousand Seconals. Now that has to be a mild form of insanity."

"People drop in," I said. This was one of the few times I had seen her smile since she started sleeping on the couch across from me.

"I took planes. For this period, I was running on planes. Short vacations and dope runs. Las Vegas and Scottsdale, Mexico City and Puerto Vallarta."

"Were you a hooker in all those towns?"

"No, just floating. I only hooked in L.A. and the Bay Area. I was a dreamy pillhead and addict. Never heroin. Coke, yes, and all kinds of hash and grass. I had troubles over the grass and hash and the LSD and the countless pills. Pills became my game, because they could be prescribed and I had the money. Finally I became so sick I was no longer able to sleep with men, became fed up with men anyway. Originally I liked men, always have. Have no bad feelings for the man at the picket fence or my mother's sharp-looking ex-husband, who broke me in and is dead anyway. They're all searching for love. I'm sure that's my bag. I searched for love, ended up loving pills and alcohol. I wanted a hero, a real man who loved only me. All I found were gray-haired old men and chemicals.

"Joe, my back aches from sitting up. I want to rest."

She lay back on the couch and I asked, "Do you want any chocolate? I'm making some."

"Yes. Put some sugar in it. Make it really sweet."

Later that night she made some changes to her story. Her mother was part Indian. Although she came from Wyoming, her family originally came from New Mexico. She indicated that her Indian blood might explain the slanty cast to her eyes, that many Indians have an Oriental cast to their eyes. This time she said her blonde hair came from her Irish and Danish ancestors.

Sandy also told me that two stepfathers had violated her, and that she also had to stay clear of a nutty, obsessed uncle and how the kids at high school kept trying to grab her ass. She said she was tall at the age of fifteen and always had a good shape but was a little slim for some people. She had grown up waiting for torna-does and cyclones and when they came heading for a shelter. But she had to be careful never to end up in the shelter alone with her stepfather or her kooky uncle. Her mother was so inadequate, so dreamy and a liar and dependent on men that she never sided with Sandy but always believed the man's side. Sandy had always attracted older men and did feel a gap between herself and her own generation. Maybe that's why she ended up in prostitution. She didn't understand the full connotation. She concluded that sex was only a physical thing and not emotional, that she did it just for money, like a job. She tried to leave her emotions home when she went to work and tried to pick them up again when she came home. She tried to live like a normal everyday young lady after a day of paid sex but ultimately found she could not.

"I've known girls who have had pimps," she said. "One girl I knew, Sharon Lee, said that pimps aren't always terrible exploiters of women. Her father supported her mother her whole life, and he was the breadwinner. She thought a lot of these relationships were no worse than if the woman's the breadwinner. Of course there's a lot of tragic ones, too."

"When the breadwinner doesn't want to be the breadwinner, that's what's tragic," I said.

"Right," Sandy said. "There are exploitive relationships in this world, and sometimes pimps are one of those exploitive relationships. But you can also find those in other walks of life."

"There's no middle ground for me," I said. "Pimps are pukey parasites."

She continued about her life. The Bay Area was easier than L.A. She kept an apartment and didn't take outcalls and became adept at spotting trouble. She listened to the tone of voice and the questions on the phone and decided if the client was safe. For some reason she was never bothered by the vice squad. Maybe because she kept a low profile, she thought. Whenever she tried to leave the life and work as a waitress, her feet got tired and her arms ached from the piles of dishes. And men made passes at her even then. Working in a supermarket meant long hours, and she got tired at night so went back to hooking. Either way her life was unsatisfactory.

She needed an edge so she explored grass and then cocaine and then pills because doctors prescribed them so easily. When she finally found booze with pills, she numbed her mind, and stroking six or seven older men in the afternoons seemed easier. That nothing is free, she discovered the hard way. There was a price tag on everything.

And after she left Haight Street, she wandered to southern California to crash the movies but ended up working as a carhop. She lived in Venice, across from the beach in a pad above a garage. She lived with one of the beach bums, a weightlifter, but she didn't trust younger men. She knew how to handle older men. They were easier to manage and less demanding. Her hair was very long at the time, and because she lived near the beach and swam a lot, she was deeply tanned. She wore kooky sunglasses and had the same leggy shape she had now.

An affair with a man who owned a donut shop on the boardwalk resulted in an abortion. A painful, grisly weekend in Tijuana. The abortion and an agency for young, lost, and unfortunate girls led to an involvement with a therapist who was a Jungian. The therapist became lost in her dreams and her shape and her youth—and her fast and silly girlish way of using slang from the movies.

"Remember I was only nineteen years old, and this guy had my head glowing. He said I looked glamorous and lost, with my Mary Pickford curls. He had me reading Esther Harding and Camus."

"Anyone who will read Camus will eat frog legs," I said.

"Joe, don't joke. I was nutty in those days."

"What part of these stories is true?"

"They're all kinda true."

"The stories are also kinda contradictory," I said.

"Truthfully, my past is zilch. My past is not important."

"Don't tell me anymore of where you've been or what you've done. All these childhood fantasies and love affairs with therapists and older men and the time you spent as a hippie or a hooker have no meaning to me. They're like political buttons on someone's jacket so you know who they are. I'd rather figure you out on my own."

We didn't talk much more. Although she didn't avoid me, we no longer talked all night or during most of the day. When she sat by herself, a couple of guys hit on her. All the counselors hung around and gave her an inordinate amount of attention. The women steered clear of her. I knew why. As the glow came back to her cheeks and she pressed her clothes, her style and looks became out of place in the detox. But when it was time to eat, she always waited for me. We sat next to each other, and if she found a book of matches, she gave them to me. Tobacco and matches were at a premium in this place.

When Monte came by with his usual package of goodies for me, I introduced them. I noticed he called her kid or kiddo. That was another of Monte's affected styles. He did ask if she needed stockings and said he'd bring some on his next trip. She mentioned she had some money and a few clothes at a friend's house. She had a promise of a job as a waitress in a downtown bar and grill if she had the energy to hold it.

At night she spent part of the time listening to the music with me, then slept on the couch. I stayed up, smoked, and caught a few catnaps. The staff was determined to place me into some sobriety program, but I insisted that I had a job. I promised to join AA or go to the therapy groups at Garden Sullivan or even to the Gestalt Center. Sandy was slated for Laguna Honda. She was still exhausted and weak. She needed a few weeks' recuperation and sobriety before she could handle running around with a stack of dishes in some restaurant.

On the morning I checked out, she stood close to me. I kissed her lightly on the cheek, told her to take care of herself. I didn't ask if she wanted me to check on her in Laguna Honda. We had told each other our stories and had commiserated with each other. We had staved off the loneliness of the nights. Now it was time to go our own ways. Besides, I was twenty years older, in a way old enough to be her father. I didn't want to be plugged into her dream machine. Beauty is a highly perishable item, and her time was short. I knew that I'd never see her again.

Sometimes I was able to delude myself that I was not a loser, knowing that everyone in the Valencia detox was a loser. Sandy had not strayed in here accidentally, a young, shapely, articulate girl on her way up. She was a loser, too. She was a girl with loose thighs, looking for something and hoping to get it via her body. Waiting for the knight on the white charger, and he wasn't coming. Me . . . I'm trying to go the distance, but I'm hep that nobody wins. When I walked out the door, I noticed the swingy young counselor moving in to give Sandy comfort and advice.

IV *The* India Opera *and the Rats*

Monte sat back with his feet propped on the desk. As he smoked the big cigar, he stroked it like a woman's leg, sending smoke rings toward the ceiling. Piles of paper on the desk. Unanswered letters. Not that he was slow or didn't take care of business, but he drowned in papers. What the hell had they ever done before the typewriter or the copy machine? The girls typed the letters, but he still had to read them and dictate. You went to work on the docks to escape this avalanche of paper, but there was no escape.

His lips tugged gently on the cigar. Slowly he thumbed through the small blue book, the last contract. What looks like a stone wall to a layman becomes a triumphal arch to a corporation lawyer. Where had he picked up that line? The pitfalls, the triple meanings of the words. A few years ago being a business agent was a bonanza—dress up, wander around the docks, a few good words here and there. Now it was exhausting. It demanded a lawyer.

The endless procession of problems. An arbitration this morning. Another beef in Oakland on the use of the cage. Phoning the Pacific Maritime Association—the PMA—on two men shorted of their pay. The gangs in the hatch over in Richmond, working steel shorthanded. Visiting Boone in the nutward at San Francisco General. What did Boone want? Wanted to learn Cantonese and how to play the ukelele. Carney coming to work this morning— lucky to be out on a suspended sentence—and his car wouldn't start. He went back into the house, came out with a .45, and pumped five slugs into the engine block. From what scenario, what new mystique for solving a problem?

Between puffs on the cigar, Monte decided that he was the trustee for the dead and the absent, trustee for the walking wounded. His finely honed political instincts were of little use. He couldn't defuse any more situations. Joe could conceal himself behind booze. All Monte had was his conscience. Suddenly he stopped and a smile brightened his face. He ran a hand through his wavy brown hair. He was beginning to take himself seriously. When you begin to believe your own bullshit, you're really in trouble, he decided.

Monte shifted papers around, making a quick attempt to bring order to his desk. He locked the drawer where he kept his important and private items. Adjusting his fedora, carrying his London Fog raincoat over his arm, he locked the door of the B.A.'s office. One last chore for tonight . . . the Albany City Jail. He had to bail Zack out for being drunk and disorderly at Golden Gate Racetrack. Since Monte had decided to run for the presidency of Local 10, he knew he had to run hard and he had to win. He did not intend to be blindsided by the same bombs anymore.

In the morning Monte handled his first beef. As he walked between the pier sheds, he saw that the entire ship had been shut down. No gear moving and all the gangs standing by.

"What's the beef?" he asked Siberia Sam.

"Forty-one rats spotted in one hour in hatch four."

"Where's the ship from?"

"India," Siberia Sam said. "The ship's named the *India Opera*. I hit one rat with a potato, and it squealed like a soprano."

Siberia Sam was one of the few lefties with a sense of humor. Monte had a good feel for him. Siberia Sam was reasonable. Another alki, same as Joe. Monte knew him to be one of Joe's running mates. He had been a good winch driver until the booze got to him.

"You working that hatch?" he asked Siberia Sam.

"No . . . but when they fired Walter's gang, we refused to replace them. What are you going to do?"

"If forty-one rats are visible in one hour in a hatch, then I'm going to shut the ship down. No way out . . . the shipowners have to fumigate the entire ship."

"I hit another of the bastards with a potato, and it flew off a beam."

"Potatoes in the hatch . . . in a cooler?" Monte asked.

"No, nuts of some kind. Cashews or walnuts. Curry in some cases. There are some barrels, the same kind that carries pickles or molasses, but I don't know what's in them."

Hatch four. Walter's gang. An old-time gang. The four regular holdmen, Hawaiians. Two good winch drivers, Max and a Black called Drifty.

Walter talking rapidly. "The place is crawling with rats. We saw them soon as we opened the hatch. And they were bold, running out in the open. I figured once we started working, the rats'd disappear into the bilges . . . no such luck. I called the men up. Then they sent the U-Boat Commander's gang down, and they wouldn't go. The Commander's gang is over there . . . offshore."

Monte called the Commander over. He spoke to both the gang bosses. "If you refuse to go down, it's a violation of the contract."

"The contract's got a lot of holes in it," Walter said. "But it's clear on health and safety. If it jeopardizes our health or our safety, we just stand by and call the B.A."

"How about you?" Monte asked the U-Boat Commander.

"Yoost as Walter say, health and safety."

"How come all the questions?" Walter asked.

"I want to hear you say it. Health and safety loud and clear. Here comes Carava and the pipsqueak Gamboa."

Jim Carava, the pier superintendent, big and blustery, almost six foot eight inches tall, and running beside him the walking boss Gamboa, who was short and thin and had a high reedy voice that became frantic whenever he wanted to get a point across.

"Health and safety," Monte said.

"Did you see any rats?" Carava asked.

"Not yet. I was waiting for you."

They went to the coaming together. The rest of the men from the two gangs crowded the coaming, now joined by an additional gang from hatch five. The entire coaming was ringed with men.

Monte took off his fedora and held it in his hand as he leaned forward. Nothing. Carava and Gamboa flanked him. One of the holdmen from Walter's gang made a motion to sail his white cap down into the hatch, but Monte motioned to him by holding up his hand to indicate no. One rat on a beam, black and long with the tail dragging on the beam. Jerky skippy moves, kangaroo moves, hoppy. Another, larger than the first. Three more. That made five on the beam. Walter pointed to two rats running across the boxes of curry, disappearing, their tails whips as they zooped into the spaces between the boxes. More rats.

"That's enough for me," Monte said. "This ship has to be fumigated."

"That's not enough for me," Carava said. "I'm ordering the other gang to go down."

"Which gang?" Monte asked. "Are we going to play musical gangs?"

"The gang from hatch five."

"Do we have to go through each gang?" Monte said. "Not a single gang will go down. And if they wanted to, I wouldn't allow them. I'm knocking the ship off on a health and safety beef. Please read me loud and clear. Health and safety. No man has to work in a hatch with forty rats. The place is crawling with them. If we saw this many from the coaming, there must be hundreds. Why don't we handle this fast?" He pointed to Gamboa. "You worked cargo. Would you go into the hatch?"

"I was down in the hatch. The men called me down," Gamboa answered in his squeaky voice. It was obvious to Monte that he was trying to avoid the question. Although all the walking bosses were originally longshoremen, after they bought split-level houses and big cars they became part of management. Fence straddlers. Sometimes they even used the language of the left, talked radical, and camouflaged their loyalties. Monte had seen it happen. The good walkers in the port could be counted on one hand. Maybe he should not be so severe . . . for sure, half the walkers had gone highrise, Gamboa among them.

"I'm calling the arbitrator," Carava said.

One of the longshoremen said, "Call your mother."

"I think it might be wiser if you called the exterminator," Monte said.

The gangs stood by until the arbitrator came: Frank Hollard, a short man in a dark suit and a white shirt with a tab collar that had gone out of style ten years ago. Black pointy shoes. He resembled a funeral director. A stubborn man who constantly ran his hands through his fringe of gray hair. He walked with short running steps, and the longshoremen nicknamed him "Foxtrot." Monte lit a cigar, his eyes glossing over the No Smoking signs. Monte blew a puff of smoke that obscured the sign.

The arbitrator was inside the clerk's shack calling on the phone. Monte, still smoking the cigar, waited for all the calls to be made,

the people to be consulted, the decisions . . . Why all the trouble?
A quick turnaround meant money. Each extra day at the dock cost
a bundle. Fumigation itself was expensive, and some cargo loss
due to fumigation was to be expected. Money versus the health
and safety of the longshoremen. There could be no compromise,
no choosing of sides. Monte knew he couldn't back down; the ship
had to be fumigated. It was so clear to him as he waited, puffing
on his cigar, his eyes going over the signs on the dock. On the side
of the shed in big white letters, white house paint, the letters
close to three feet high: REMEMBER CHARLIE. The longshoreman who always ran for dispatcher and always lost. *Todos gringos
es maricones.* Someone doubted the manhood of the North Americans. The FBI investigated cargo thefts. Why didn't they investigate
the rats?

Frank Hollard came out of the clerk's shack. "I'm not making
any decisions. I called the Department of Agriculture. They'll
be down."

"Should the men stand by?" Monte asked.

"The gangs are all fired," Carava said. "No work, no pay."

Monte considered his options. If they stood by, the men would
ease off a few at a time. Who knew when the government men
might arrive? Monte told the men to go home. He went back to
his office.

Later in the afternoon, Monte received a call from the arbitrator,
and another call five minutes later from Carava. The government
men had caught two rats in hatch three and another in the adjoining
hatch. Autopsied or whatever they did with dead rats. The Department of Agriculture's verdict: The rats did not have the plague.
There were no sick crew members on the ship. These were good
rats, and the men had to work the ship.

As soon as Monte put down the phone from Carava's call, he
dialed the chief dispatcher. "Shedly, this is Monte. They say the
rats are good rats. Please hear me. Be sure to dispatch the exact
amount of gangs the shipowners want for the *India Opera.* Yes,
Pier Thirty-two, on the face. I'll be in the dispatch hall in the
morning. The men should know that they will go to the ship, but
they are not to work it. I'm shutting down the ship, contract with
PMA, government men, or not. I don't care what they say. No
man is working that ship even if I have to hire a professional

ratcatcher and pile a mountain of dead rats near the gangway. I'll burn the rats in front of the newspaper reporters." Then he called the *San Francisco Chronicle* and the *San Francisco Examiner*. Carefully he explained the exact nature of the problem. Although he asked both papers to send reporters to the pier, he was not sure they would.

Monte made the announcement in the hall during the morning dispatch. A coterie of his friends and good union men volunteered for the jobs on the *India Opera*. When Monte went down to the pier, all the gangs dispatched to the job were there, including his old gang, the gang now held by the Duke of Cream Sherry. The Duke was walking back and forth with his hands behind his back, his stringy hair uncombed, and his long overcoat dragging on the cement of the pier. Monte saw his brother Joe. Dark sunglasses. That usually meant Joe was on one of his runs, but today Joe was laughing and joking with his clique—Borrego Red, Roger, Nanakule John, Siberia Sam, and Eddie Tijera, who wore a natty Tahitian sport shirt and had a knife-edge crease in his khakis. Roger showed Monte a small revolver.

"Who's that for, the arbitrator?" Monte asked.

"I'm gonna potshot some rats," Roger said.

"That's not cool," Monte said. "Put it away. We have enough trouble."

Jim Carava faced Monte. "Send the men aboard," he ordered.

"No," Monte said.

Carava screaming something about the Department of Agriculture, that there was no longer a health problem.

"Fumigate the ship," Monte said. "If not, let the PMA and the government men work the ship, because no longshoremen from Local 10 are going aboard."

Carava rushed to the clerk's shack. In a few minutes, Monte's beeper came on. Return to the office.

When Monte arrived at the Longshoremen's Hall, he was intercepted by Merle, the vice president, a young light-skinned Black who had high goals in the union. Merle was acting president, as Judniken, the president of Local 10, was in the East for a parley with the hierarchy of the ILA. Merle, a college man who had a modulated voice, carefully selected his words. "They are using the grieved-ship part of the contract. If we don't work the specific grieved ship, the shipowners can shut down the rest of the port. They can do this, you know."

"I know they can," Monte said. "But they can't get away with it."

The rest of the morning Monte stayed in his office. The International called. He informed them that he would take care of the rat beef at the local level. The spokesman for the coast committee said that he better. Monte knew he did not need the International and their pussyfooted way of compromise. No, Jesus Christ, he did not need them. Many men milling around Monte's office and congratulating him. One longshoreman shaking his fist at Monte, more than hinting that Monte received his pay from the longshoremen. If they lost their pay across the entire port, why didn't he lose his?

Smoking a cigar, the brim of his fedora pulled down low so no one could see his eyes, his feet on the desk, sending smoke rings that diffused on the ceiling, Monte sat and waited. More calls from the PMA and the International. Merle, the vice president, bugging him but never intimating that the men should go back to work. A call from the Seaman's Union congratulating him for shutting down a foreign ship. Calls from his wife.

At three o'clock he went to see if the shipowners had ordered nightgangs for the *India Opera*. No. Monte told Shedly to be sure to fill all the gangs for the *India Opera* tomorrow. Then he went back to his office and ordered the men out. He hung his suitcoat on a hanger, put his fedora on the desk, rolled up his sleeves. Slowly he went through the *Chronicle*, then the *Examiner*. Nothing about the rats. Opening a desk drawer, he took out a fifth of VO. With a fancy pocketknife, he cut away the celluloid and twisted off the cap. He filled a small four-ounce water glass half full. He held his hand steady. No tremor. He downed the drink.

The next morning, after the men refused to go aboard the *India Opera*, the PMA shut down the port. In the afternoon, the ship moved to the Fourteenth-Street Pier in Oakland, across the bay. Monte was informed that the ship had ordered nightgangs. Monte followed the ship and waited for the nightgangs. Eddie Tijera came with him. The night longshoremen refused to work the grieved hatch. When Monte came off the pier with the rest of the longshoremen, a reporter caught up with him.

"We heard about the rats."

"Where were you yesterday or the day before?" Monte asked.

"Hey, Mister Karsten, give me a chance. We don't run the newspaper."

Monte gave the reporter a concise history and highlights of the so-called rat story. Then he pulled the reporter close, holding him by the lapels. "Put this in and highlight it word for word."

"We better go over by the streetlight," the reporter said.

Monte talking. "If you were a mother, would you want your son to work a ship where forty-one rats were spotted in a one-hour period, knowing the ship comes from a country where there is cholera? If you were a daughter, would you want your father to work a ship that is rat infested, understanding that the ship comes from a typhus-ridden country? If you were a wife, would you want your husband to work a ship crawling with rats, totally out of control? And the ship comes from a country that is explosive in epidemics and has the highest rate of plague in the world. Would anyone want some workingman who is dear to them to work this rat-ridden ship, the *India Opera*, while they are conscious of the fact that the shipowners and the representatives of the federal government refuse to have the ship fumigated and decontaminated?"

The next morning the front page of the *Chronicle* carried the story of the rats. Monte saw that the story asked his questions of every mother, daughter, and wife. The editorial page had a full cartoon of a small longshoreman hunched over, protecting his lunchbucket with his body. Hovering over him was a gigantic rat holding a cargo hook above its head, ready to plunge the hook into the back of the longshoreman. That afternoon, the *India Opera* sailed for the port of Vancouver in Canada. Monte called the president of the Vancouver local and told him of the port shutdown by the PMA. Monte emphasized the solidarity of the longshoremen of San Francisco Local 10.

After the call, Monte went to Ginsburg's Dublin Pub on Bay Street, two blocks from the hall. "A double VO," he said. Taking a cigar from his pocket, he stroked the cigar, then lit it. The beautiful dark tobacco came from the Canary Islands. It cost one dollar and five cents. The olive-skinned cigar makers spent ten hours a day over the cigar boards. Their dreams were wrapped into the unique expressiveness of the cigar. Monte's dreams? Monte knew there would be no arbitration, no fines, no trouble from International.

And Monte knew he had stepped onto the first rung of the ladder leading to the presidency of the local next November.

Our Lady of Sorrows—the large red-brick building surrounded by grass and protected by a high black picket fence. Monte threw his cigar on the lawn as he climbed the stairs. Charlie, the president of the Pensioners Club, had filled in the blanks on Sean Reilly. Reilly was not dead. Reilly was sick. How sick Monte did not know. On his deathbed? Perhaps. The nun at the desk sent Monte to the third floor.

Monte searched along the corridor and then the long room. No other patients. Sean Reilly was in the last bed partially obscured by a curtain. He was a barrel-chested man, big in his days as a gang boss but propped up in bed now—skin over bones. The chest still big in the rib cage, but no fat or muscle left. The head large and the eyes rheumy. Thinning hair and his forehead glistening. Tubes lay beside the bed, but none in Reilly's nose. Equipment next to the bed with countless dials. A bottle held on a metal stand with tubes leading to his arm. Whenever he took a breath, his chest heaved, and if he coughed, his chest sounded as if liquid sloshed around inside.

Monte held a fresh cigar in his mouth, but it wasn't lit.

"No smoking, lad," Reilly said. His eyes pierced the foreground, trying to focus on Monte. Reilly indicated the oxygen tanks beside the bed but back near the wall.

"It's me. Monte."

Reilly tried to focus, then motioned for Monte to come closer. No doubt about it, the old man was having trouble breathing.

"What's the matter? Heart attack?"

Reilly motioned Monte even closer, until their heads were only inches apart. "I guess this is about the end of it, lad."

A series of coughs. Reilly's chest heaving and afterward with trembling hands brushing his mouth with a small white towel.

"Emphysema," Reilly said.

They sat for a few minutes, neither of them talking. Monte remembered the old Irish gang boss from his better days, a tough-talking old Irishman who loved to drink. A chain smoker. Reilly smoked one cigarette after another, crumbled the empty packs, and threw them into the water between the pier and the hulk of the ship. Reilly never wore the longshore uniform. Monte never recalled him wearing a Hickory shirt or a white cap. Reilly wore old suitcoats that never matched the pants. Always a sweat-stained fedora and on cold days a knitted khaki sweater under his suitcoat.

Reilly visited Ireland every four or five years. Whenever he came back from Ireland and whenever Monte caught his gang as a winch driver, they talked of these trips. Reilly never mentioned Irish history or the lure of relics. Monte was not sure he had ever visited a historical site or even knew about the Abbey Theatre. Reilly's trips were simple. Take a hotel room near the docks of Cork. Begin the day with stiff slugs of Irish whiskey. Then break-fast, in what Monte assumed to be some form of Irish cafeteria, and take a brisk stroll along the docks and chat with the dock-workers. A busman's holiday.

Reilly had no problem with identity. His entire carriage indicated a workingman who spent a lifetime on the docks of Cork and San Francisco. A few good drinks and a good argument with his wife, a little money in the bank and the ever-present pack of Cam-els, the thick Irish fingers ripping the top from the pack like a bear ripping the cap from a jar of honey. If he had an argument on the docks, he stood nose to nose with the man and screamed him down.

Monte's eyes went over the tubes, the bottle of oxygen, the machinery, and the variety of dials. So this is where the old man had steered his life.

Monte leaned close, his lips inches from Reilly's ear. "Sean, you will live to piss on my grave."

The old man tried to muster a smile, but it was too difficult. He lay there with his chest moving up and down, sucking at the air. Talking was difficult.

"Do you want me to visit you again?"

"If you wish, lad."

"Can I bring you anything? A bottle of booze?" That brought a slight smile to the Irishman's face. Monte almost asked if he wanted a pack of Camels, but he checked himself. What could he say? The old man didn't talk, no reminiscences, no good old times, only the stare into the horizon of death.

"What can I bring you?" Monte asked again.

"Only my health, and I know you can do nothing of that, lad."

Monte took the old man's hand and held it. He caressed the hand in an affectionate and loving way. "I'll be back tomorrow," he said. Then he walked rapidly from the room.

The long corridor smelled of antiseptic and death. Plaster statues at every corner and in every niche—Jesus, Saint Mary, Saint Theresa. Cold, inhuman place, Monte decided. Better to be up in Kaiser Hospital with most of the other longshoremen. Kaiser did not give as much personal attention, but at least he'd be with old friends. Why was he so isolated and alone? No one else in the room of the convalescent home, only oxygen tanks and saints.

When Monte came down to the second landing, an older woman in a wheelchair pivoted close to him. He tried to pass her, but her trembling and surprisingly strong hand deterred him. There were seven women sitting on the bench and a half-dozen women in wheelchairs, all old, some with bandages on their heads or wrists. The woman held him.

"Take me home," she said.

"I can't take you home, mom," he said.

"They're holding me here. I have money." She fumbled in the pocket of her apron. "I have a place to go. My apartment. They are keeping me here. They won't let me go. I want to go home," she insisted.

"Is she supposed to be here?" Monte asked the other women in general. One woman giggled childishly; two others whispered to each other.

"I can't take you out of here. Do you have any children?" he asked the woman who clutched his sleeve.

"I have no children," she said. Her mouth puckered, drawn into small thin lips. She had no teeth, real or false.

Monte hesitated for a moment. The newspapers always had reports of older men and women in nuthouses and recovery homes, virtually held prisoners with no one to intercede for them. People discarded in the final years of their lives, buried for the remainder of their years. But this was a well-known Catholic convalescent home, open to the public. The woman was not locked in some small cell. She was free to wheel around, stop whomever she liked. Monte did not relish unclear situations.

He extricated himself from the clamped fingers. "Mom, I'm

going to check with the people at the desk." She grabbed his sleeve again. Carefully trying not to twist her fingers, he took her hand away. "Please be nice. I am going to check for you."

The nurse at the main desk in the lobby raised her head, stopped writing on a chart. She had on a white cap with a blue cross directly in the center of the cap. Slender shoulders and long-trimmed manicured nails. Red hair. Even under the cap, Monte could see that her hair was straight. Green eyes and a play of a smile at the corner of her lips. The name Katherine printed on a plastic badge.

"Are you in charge?" Monte asked.

"I am the nurse on this shift. Can I help you?"

"I don't know how to put this. Believe me, I'm not looking for trouble. There is a woman on the second floor. Well, she stopped me and said she was being held here. She wanted to go home. That she had enough money and she wanted to go home. That is, not stay here anymore."

"Did she have her teeth out?"

"Yes."

"That would be Molly."

"That she didn't have any children, but that she had enough money and wanted to go home," Monte said.

"Molly tells bloody fibs, she does." The English accent easy to identify. "Not that she hasn't enough money. That she has. Boodles of it. Her family. Four children. One was here earlier. And you may not give credence to me, but she has her very own lawyer. Not her children's lawyer, but her very own. The Mother Superior is her cousin. Shall I refer you to her?"

Monte began to smile. The nurse smiled, too, and with her fingers she touched Monte's hand. "Please believe me. We are not holding her a bloody prisoner. Please believe that."

"Another question?" Monte said. "I'm the business agent for the longshoremen. Sean Reilly on the third floor is one of our pension-ers. Is he on his last legs? Is this about the end of it for him?"

"No, it is not the end of it. Mr. Reilly is not a healthy man, neither is he on the edge of death. He has an infection in his chest."

"Emphysema?"

"Yes, he has emphysema and a trace of diabetes. But it is the infection that has him bedridden. And it is receding. I am sure he will be released. If there was anyone competent to take care of him at home, he would well be home. His wife was here this morning. You, for one, would wonder. Incredible carrying on, swearing from the both of them, that might make a dockworker shudder. I hope you are satisfied that we are not detaining Mr. Reilly?"

"No, I know he can leave. Only checking. I will be back. Tomorrow or the next day."

"A longshore official," she said, half amused.

"What's so funny about that?"

"My uncle was a wharfie in London. I am from London. He wanted to fix me with a young dockworker. I was bloody bored with the entire arrangement."

"Are you bloody bored now?" Monte asked.

She smiled. "No. I find you rather attractive, in an old-fashioned sort of way."

Monte took a card from his pocket. "This is my work address and phone number. On your day off, give me a call. I'll give you a tour of the docks. If you play your cards right, I may buy you lunch."

Monte walked from the building. Outside the iron picket gate, he stopped. Faint heart never won fair lady, he thought. Skipping up the stairs two at a time, he went back to the desk.

"What time do you get off shift?"

"Three o'clock," she said.

"I will be parked outside at three. A black Cadillac. Sort of a racketeer's car, though I'm not a racketeer. I'm a soft and easy man to please. I favor women with red hair and green eyes. And when a man is over forty, nurses are at a premium. I will drive you home. We can drop off for a drink on the way."

He left her stunned. As he started his car, he looked at his wrist watch. One o'clock. He still had time to visit Smitty up in the detox ward at U.S. Public Health.

Monte sat at the bar of the Jackson Square Bar and Grill. He had taken Katherine out for the last two evenings, and now he was waiting for her. Many chores today. The dispatch scene. Kaiser Hospital . . . two coronaries, then visiting Hamburger, the doctors trying to lower his blood sugar.

The dockmen at Pier Fifty today, laughing at the cage setup. Sometimes the longshoremen reminded him of little kids. The way they became hysterical, laughing at the lash ships. Stupid shipowners. Driving hard to mechanize the port—experimenting—baroque gooney setups. The longshoremen laughing, splitting their sides with laughter. Monte knew better. There was a method to the shipowners' madness. The mechanization contracts had been in only for seven years. Already, the tonnage had increased by more than one hundred percent, and the total man-hours had decreased.

The *Hawaiian Fisherman*. Years ago it was a milk-run ship that make a trip to Honolulu every three weeks and always worked six days and five nights whenever it was in port. Six full gangs working every shift and eleven full shifts. Carrying all the peanuts, beer, Tampax, and cargo necessary for the supermarkets and drugstores and dime stores of Honolulu to survive. Fourteen men to a gang, a gang for each of the six hatches, and all the backup men that were needed plus the clerks and walking bosses and the supercargo. Literally an army of men for all the handjive cargo.

Monte remembered that a week ago the *Hawaiian Fisherman* had come into Encinal across the bay in Alameda. The ship tied up at one o'clock. Four crane drivers. Sixteen men aboard ship throwing the lashing off the vans. Four dockmen standing by to make sure the vans locked on the flatbeds of the trucks as they came from ship to dock. Eight men driving the flatbed trucks. Smooth as silk. A van every three or four minutes. Two traveler cranes, back and forth. Two hundred vans in less than four hours, and less than forty men for the entire ship.

Compound this by fifty ships. The ships becoming bigger, the machinery more sophisticated, the work more automated. Ten years from now San Francisco would be a ghost port. The only thing that kept them going now was the fracas in Vietnam and the plunder from Japan. Monte watched the highrises and condominiums creeping closer to the docks, the deserted piers destined to be marinas or tourist playlands. Soon the whole show would be over. A cadre of a thousand men could service the entire port. Where would that leave the other five thousand?

Katherine, the nurse from Our Lady of Sorrows, her arms bulging with packages, came through the door. She had just come from work and was still in her nurse's uniform. Why was he so turned on by women in white dresses? What was the erotic significance of white? He remembered his first trip to the convention in L.A., waiting for Shedly in front of the Roosevelt Hotel. The blonde rolling down Hollywood Boulevard with her Marilyn Monroe walk, gold hair coiled and bouncy in the sun. Her white manicurist's dress tight and grooved against the curves of her body, unhampered breasts and strong thighs. A surfer's tan. The castanet click of her high heels on the pavement. On her way to work.

Monte had tipped his straw hat. "How are you, young lady?" he had said.

"I'm fine, old man," she retaliated.

Shedly had come up, watching her rear end and firm calves as she cut across the street. "I'd love to bite her on the ass, get lockjaw, and have her drag me to death," he said.

"Are you dreaming?" Katherine asked, interrupting his reverie.

Katherine's apartment was located above the Stockton Tunnel across from Cogswell College. Heavy traffic on the streets, the clanging of the Powell Street cable cars, fire engines in the night, the shriek of an ambulance, police cars, the noxious smell of exhaust from the tunnel. An occasional firecracker from Chinatown. The strong salt air, the vapors of fog, the million-windowed city, and the string of lights from the San Francisco–Oakland Bay Bridge.

Monte closed the windows to shut out the noise. The simple, chaste apartment with its wooden bed in one corner and the stereo with the two speakers. The comfortable chairs and the splash of color in the bedspread, the blue curtains, and the checkerboard slick floor of the kitchen. All the instruments of the kitchen in order. The blue enamel stove, the subdued table lamps, the teapot on a hot plate with two porcelain cups, one on either side. Roses and carnations intermingled in the squat bowl.

Outside, the smell of gasoline, the exhaust from the streets, the dead-fish smell of the docks with their mildewed, rotten wood, the sulfur smell of chemicals, like rotten eggs. Pistol shots, cars squealing around corners, the snap of cable wires. By contrast, the apartment had the smells of tea and cinnamon, roses and carnations, the subtle perfume of Katherine as he held her close.

For one second he thought of Pamela with her gray pageboy hair, bony slim body, the countryside horsey look. Monte had always gone for tough-looking women: hairdressers with their peroxided hair and false eyelashes; manicurists, rigid and pumped full of gossip; waitresses with bunioned feet and runs in their stockings. Not Pamela. She was a lady.

Now he was back with his own. The short, redheaded Katherine, with her thin slightly bandied legs. The swingy, tough-acting, jokey style. A thin, streetwise woman from the Paddington side of London, with its crisscross of ancient streets and child molesters. The bubbling teapot, the fresh smell of her hair, the way she stroked against his crotch with her thigh.

"Do you want tea, my darling?" Katherine asked.

"Not now, later." Monte assembled the bottles from the brown shopping bag. A bottle of VO and a bottle of Boodles gin. The shot glass she had bought for twenty cents. He took a short stem of a previously lit cigar, held a match to it. "Do you mind if I smoke?"

"My honey, the big ashtray by the table is your very own. The bloody Indians started this whole racket of smoking. Can't be un-American. Not at this late date. You can do whatever you like, and to me, too." She pulled him close and slid her tongue into his mouth. Then pulled away, just as suddenly. Straightening her skirt. "I shall behave myself," she said, laughing, exposing teeth, white and slightly irregular. "At least until we have tea."

Monte thinking . . . that all women were sisters under the skin was simply not true . . . that he had married the wrong woman.

Women who were compatible and agreeable in bed, just generally agreeable in relationships, were not like streetcars. If you missed one, there might not be another around the corner. Like Joe, crying over memories of that flashy Portuguese broad who left him cold and flat. Now Joe's entire life was at the bottom of a bottle. For what? A woman who could care less. And Pamela, with her neatly pressed underwear. Always wore a slip, even camisoles. Never any sex in the morning or in the afternoon or on the ground at a picnic or at a beach. Only sex at night, and in bed. A few preliminary investigations of their bodies, a mechanical contrivance. A short epileptic dance in the darkness of their bedroom. At the exact moment that he came, the look on her face, the ethereal look of a theology student.

The headaches. Pamela's constant headaches were clichés. As an expert booby-trapper himself, surely he was adept at spotting traps. Then one night, perhaps the location of the moon or as her payoff for a Joseph Magnin frock or to preserve the proprieties of marriage, short and nerve-racking sex. After he came, her disgusting habit of wrapping herself in a floater, disappearing into the bathroom, the running water, soap. Washing away what? Sin? Sperm?

Whereas Katherine. She approached sex straight on, like a woman going to a gunfight. Her dance into perfume and flesh, echoes, spasms and moans, lip on lip, flesh on flesh, her tongue a prying membrane. The random biting, squeezing, touching until his prick became as hard as a shackle pin, an adolescent frenzy. Monte began to smile. Jesus Christ, why must he take himself so seriously. Others must feel the same way.

"Did you love that, my dearest?" Katherine asked.

"You were wonderful," Monte said. He pulled her close to him, his fingers gently caressing her spine, her back. He saw the moon framed in the window. The moon was full.

"Is that the best you ever had?"

"The best."

"The very best?"

"Absolutely."

"I love doing all those crazy kinky things."

"And I love you to do them."

"Your body's so strong. It must be that bloody pushing of boxes on the dock. Love all that power, that gentleness that comes close to spiritual."

"We have it made," Monte said.

"How can we bosh the whole affair up?"

"The only way we can fuck it up," Monte said, "is if I fall in love with you."

"Don't ever do that. We shall be sweethearts, forever and ever. Is that so everlastingly old-fashionend? I'm so horridly, dreadfully, absurdly, perfectly, absolutely pleased with you. See, my darling, I never uttered the word love. Do I have to wait and beg to see you?"

"You can see me anytime you want. I have no curfew on me. No curfew whatsoever."

"I love to sit around cafés."

"We can sit around cafés, all night long, if you want. Is that British?"

"I am not British, as you so declaim. I am English. The desire to lounge in cafés is not English. Before I came to America, I went to school in Geneva and Paris. They adore café life there."

"If I wanted to see you for a short time in the afternoon?"

"Whenever I'm free of the job. Come for whatever reasons you like. American women are absolutely looney over orgasms. They must be in the mood or they feel so cheated. My darling, we can use each other at our own convenience, for our own desires. Over the long haul you will satisfy me. Whatever. Whenever. You shall have my telephone at the hospital and my apartment and at the café I adore on Geary Street and at my favorite restaurant. Am I being too bold?"

"No, sensible."

"We are going to have a sensible and ravishing arrangement for two sensible and practical people. Will you ever become tired and leave me?"

"I doubt that I will. If I leave anyone it will be my wife. Currently, I see no reason for doing that. My being married should not upset any of our plans at all."

Katherine began moving her hands under the covers.

"See, he's becoming hard again. If rape is inevitable, relax and enjoy it. I'm going to ravish you."

Monte lay in bed trying to avoid thinking of Pamela and his brother Joe. His mind jumbled. Katherine purring like a kitten. He tossed around as she explored his body with her lips and tongue. Monte thinking back to his honeymoon with Pamela. . . .

They had arrived in Mexico City in the morning, and he tried to take her onto the bed. The Hotel Monte Cassino. She used every stall in the book—that she had to have her hair done, that it was too early in the morning, that someone might see them through the window. They were six floors up. All Monte saw were the palm trees and the traffic on the *Glorietas* six floors below.

Pamela was at the hairdressers on *Calle Niza*. She had had her tarot fortune read after lunch. Now she was having her hair done. Monte breezed into a bar, what might be called a B-girls bar back in the States. Young Indio waitresses and a cigarette girl with the face of a young Dolores Del Rio and the body of a *muñeca de carne*, a baby doll. Monte bought a cigar. Flashing a roll of stateside twenties, gave her a big tip that made her body tremble in her glove-tight dress. With her soft pliable lips and the brightest white teeth he had ever seen, she whispered in his ear. Quicker than one can say *"Viva Mexico"* they were at a table in the dark part of the bar. She was under the table, suction, sperm over her lips and cheeks. He was in and out of the bar in twenty minutes, no one the wiser. Puffing on the cigar, the one purchased from the girl, watching the traffic, in gray pants and a black shirt, a Panama straw hat, waiting as Pamela came down the steps, her hair frosty and spangle bright . . .

Monte began laughing. Katherine lifted her head, watching him with her green eyes, her face level with his hips.

v *Banana Dock*

I sat on the edge of my bed lacing my work shoes. Christ, how I
hated to go to work. Since my last trip to detox, I had been in
a low and downbeat mood. I understood that alcohol had a
special significance for me—a way of taking all my troubles and
compressing them into one big trouble, until finally the cure
became worse than the disease. The gray horizon. I was forty-five
years old with a life expectancy of twenty or so more years. How
was I to make it without booze? I didn't want jails or hospitals or
nuthouses or a continuing flow of dryout and detox centers. But
I was unable to fathom a life without drinking. My circle of
friends on the waterfront were all winos or drunks. I was tuned in
to their type of life. Walking by the 540 Club the other day and
hearing the jukebox from inside set up a string of memories.

As my last day of drinking receded into the past, so did all the
memories of bad times. To have just a bottle of wine with supper.
Could I stop at a few coffee royals in the morning? The truth is
I've never been able to stop. The chains of habit are too weak to
notice until they're too strong to break. I wasn't interested in
the chicken-shit, normal way of drinking. To have one highball or
one beer—a waste of time.

When I asked Carney how much he drank, he said four or five
bottles of wine a day. Quart bottles of port. How'd he drink on
weekends? "On weekends," Carney said, "I really roll." Once I
started to drink I wanted to really roll. To have the alcohol push
back the cold distant ringing in my ears. The touch of gin that
made my life palatable. Even when I went into a bar to eat and I
saw the bartender serving others a drink, saliva coated my tongue
and mouth. Even the vision of the bum the other day, with wine
sores on his face and neck, rummaging through a debris box and
dragging out a pair of broken crutches and a forlorn wig—he'd
trade them for booze—didn't deter my compulsion. The compul-

sion was never ending. I drank to go to work, and I worked to have money to drink, an exhausting circle.

The magic in a bottle of gin. Two or three hits and the world has a different color. The trees are greener, the mountains more noble. The colors of the bay, even with a dead bass floating belly up, become a deeper blue. The girls on the streets become lovelier and the traffic more subdued. If only it wouldn't trigger-mechanize a series of actions that lead to chaos. If only? Food without booze is pure cardboard. Just parking a car in a tight place is a pain in the ass—nervous juggling back and forth. A few drinks and *zappo*, a couple of bumper crunches, and the car is in place.

I'm not alone. Siberia Sam had to quit the winch board because of booze. He confided in me: "I'd never forgive myself if I dropped a pontoon on a bunch of stiffs." He was eighty-sixed out of the party because of booze. Lost his one and only love, a feisty Jewish girl whose nipples got hard at headlines. Siberia Sam handled his life much more conservatively than I did, and he was unable to handle booze. And I didn't want to think of Sweetdick when he drank. Jumping out of the car to get into fights. Honking his horn at every girl on the street. The Duke of Cream Sherry sitting alone in a movie theater with a quart of cheap sherry and a lemon cream pie. It made me sick to think of it.

I was in a double bind. I craved and needed booze, and when I got it, it no longer did what I wanted it to do. I wanted a world of no heartaches, no tears, and no pain. But . . . the constant recurrent image of the rats and the little girl angels—even sober. Sometimes in my dreams I'd hear them speak . . . they said . . . the wind has been murdered and all flights are canceled.

I dragged myself down to the car to go to work.

Borrego Red talking. "Joe, I've known you for fifteen years, and you told me six different ways you separated from your wife, and even the two times you told me she died you told me she died in different ways. Of course, since you quit drinking you don't tell as many lies."

We were standing under the corrugated roof of the shed of the banana dock on Third Street waiting for the walking boss to call out the time—"Let's go"—for us to start aboard.

I had taken a bath last night, and my clothes were clean. I had eaten a good meal last night, slept between clean sheets. Without calculating the date, I knew I'd been sober for two months. I knew I should feel good, but I didn't. An inner music, deep and disturbing and ringed with lonesomeness, pervaded my every mood.

I smoked a cigarette, Borrego Red, my partner, standing beside me. I glanced at Borrego, motionless, a statue in the mist. Borrego Red was a good partner, a hard worker, one who made hard jobs easy and easy jobs a rumba. Originally from Montana, he had been a state ranger in Southern California before becoming a longshoreman. As a ranger he had been a jeep patrolman at the Anza Borrego Desert State Park, and he had curly red hair with a trace of gray, hence the name Borrego Red. Stocky and strong, often when he drank he became a bar wrecker. Easy to underrate at every level, Borrego had a good reputation on the docks.

I looked around. Some of the other longshoremen drinking coffee out of paper cups from the Tick Tock. A few sipping cans of beer. Panel truck with stores for the crew backed up near the gangway of the ship, brown-faced seamen hurrying up the gangway with the boxes. The seamen in T-shirts in contrast to the long-shoremen in their bulky coats.

We heard the walker say, "Let's go-o-o-o." Then the longshore-men began their march up the gangway. Robot longshoremen anticipating a tough day with banana stalks taller than they were and a pushy fast rhythm of work no different from the assembly lines in Detroit.

"The shipowners wanted to try gorillas to hustle these big stalks," Borrego said. "They'd be cheaper and maybe faster than us, only they were afraid they'd eat all the bananas."

"The gorillas could double as tourists. Kick around downtown Frisco at night," I said.

"Tourists in black fur coats, without money, in this cold-assed, overpriced town," Borrego said.

"Don't be bitter," I said.

"I'm not bitter," Borrego said. "When we gonna see the sun? An' even Crabby John raised the price of his sandwiches."

I stepped from the gangway and hustled along the passageway holding onto the rail. "Use that ranger imagination. We're going down to coral beaches and soft guitars . . . Centr-a-a-a-l America. Bananas, bananas."

"We're in hatch three," Borrego said. "Last time I worked this crate, the stalks were as big as palm trees."

Borrego coming down the ladder behind me.

"Hey man, not so fucking fast," I said. "You're stepping on my hands."

The bananas on deck three and in hatch three were up to the belt. I had to edge my way in and crawl over the last few rows. There was a small, cleared area around the rectangular hole that the belt came through. There was one deck below and two working decks above us. The belt began to rotate and the pockets came up, one from the lower deck already loaded with a stalk that filled the pocket, the stalk so long that it clipped off going up, so big that it extended over each end of the pocket. Borrego had crawled in, and we were the only two clearing a section in front of the belt. I reached under the lower end of the stalk and gripped the main trunk part, held the upper end in my right hand, and then, bracing the stalk with my thighs, with a few short steps I jammed the stalk into the revolving pocket. Our speed picked up as we widened the area around the scoop, but we constantly worked a channel clear to the ladder so the other longshoremen could come through. More men working with us and the belt creaking and some stalks missing the pockets, as we began hurrying to meet the empty pockets, running and tossing the stalks. Occasionally a stalk that missed fell alongside the edge and crashed below, the longshoremen on the lower deck screaming, "Watch it assholes . . . motherfuckers, the bananas go up, not down." Or more personal from friends: "It must be Joe or that lunkhead from the sticks." Nothing slowed the pace. A stalk had jammed somewhere. Somehow quickly rectified, the belt was rotating again, rotating the pockets like some Ferris wheel taking the bananas up and over the main deck and onto the running roller lines where the men on the dock took their turns and humped them into the freight cars or the backed-up line of trucks. The squeaky belt, the constant click of the rollers, the aggravated noise of a couple of hundred men, the decks below dark and then lighter as we cleared the bananas toward the bulkhead and the lights from the ship's wings lit up our deck. Men running with stalks balanced on their thighs and their hands gripped on opposite ends of the stalks. Noise, swearing, the rackety clack of the scoop and the shadows of dark becoming lighter, and with the yellow bananas, the lower deck became a tropical vision of hell.

I have strong forearms and big hands with long fingers, and these were assets for me as I grabbed the stalks, skipped, and ran—just as I had done as an outfielder—and slammed the gigantic stalk into the pocket. As I went back for another stalk, I watched the other men. Roebling, an old-timer who had come on the waterfront after the Big Strike but before World War Two. A hard worker and not much of a buddy-buddy talker. Sweetdick, a black who teamed up with me and Borrego whenever possible, a stand-up comedian, never allowing his conversation to be channeled into race relations but into jokes and quips and conquests of women and gossip about the Fillmore area. Sweetdick was one of my many drinking partners whenever I went on a run. He was often called Sleeping Sickness, but that name rankled him. Not so Sweetdick or Lover. He never showed fatigue or talked of the longshore industry or about how the union was run. Sometimes simplistic, always generous and swearing and joshing, and whenever another longshoreman made a move toward him in jest, Sweetdick would scream, "Po . . . lee . . . ssss!" But I knew Sweetdick avoided the police and never called them. He was not scary . . . but he always packed a switchblade in his boot.

Two partners, Roger and Nanakule John. Roger Walsh, a former seaman in his early forties, good-looking in a rough Irish sort of way, black wavy hair touched with gray, a grade-A bullshitter who had been around ships so long that he made every move as if it was absorbed into his nature. His trademark: a fine, stylistic way of using stories and descriptions and slang and adventures of past times and other countries all jumbled into a stew that gave him a seawise air. Roger could hear a cork pop at three hundred yards.

Nanakule John, a big brute Hawaiian, strong as an ox, fast for his size, generally known as one of the toughest men on the front. Gentle in his conversation, agreeable, always giving everyone the edge. But he could not be pushed. If there was an argument and a fight couldn't be avoided, he went for broke, boots and hands, teeth and fists, elbows and knees. I knew him as a man who was dependable toward the job and his friends, a man who lit an occasional cigar and smoked it with relish, drank an occasional drink but never lost control. And at a party or a wedding, sometimes he'd blow a joint of grass, his brown eyes gone distant, lost on some island, some shore with lapping waves. Nanakule balanced his excesses.

In the afternoon twelve men were working on the third deck. Men took their breaks in pairs. Often only six men would be working at one time, and we had to hustle as every fourth pocket was ours. Bananas broken, and the stalks falling aside, and the deck slippery from squashed bananas, the men careful to keep from skidding or slipping. At least twice during the afternoon I slipped on the deck, barely avoiding crashing into the revolving belt and all the dangling machinery that had a reputation for crunching arms and legs. A few of the longshoremen ate bananas, but most sent out for beer or went over for a beer on their breaks. A few of the men with half-pints—a quick guzzle, grab a stalk, and run. The rhythm and tempo increased by the afternoon. A shriek, and Nanakule John grabbed Roebling by his coat collar, yanking him backward as they both skidded on the slippery deck. Roebling sat bewildered, holding his arm and elbow.

"Is it broken?" I asked.

"Naw, I don't think so," Roebling's face twisted in pain.

"Can we get the jacket off?" I asked. "Holler if it hurts." Carefully, with difficult moves, I helped Roebling squirm out of his jacket.

Rolled up his sleeve. The arm was bruised, and it was sheer luck that the gears hadn't taken it. Nanakule John had yanked Roebling free just in time. One finger was badly scraped. The arm wasn't swollen yet, but I knew this did not mean much, as Roebling's arm might be big and swollen black and blue the next morning. It had happened to me on the reefer dock in Alameda. I dropped a box of meat on my foot above the arch and worked the rest of the day. The next morning it was so swollen I couldn't put on my shoe.

The gang boss screaming from above. "Fill those pockets or hit the ladder." More screaming and the steady creak of the scoops.

Roebling had his jacket back on and was testing his bruised arm and fingers by trying to manhandle a stalk.

"Go up and report the injury," Borrego said. "Don't be foolish. Go and report it."

"Take a break," Roger said.

"Go up and report it," I said. "Then go over and have yourself a beer. Come on, no bullshit. We can handle it down here. Go on, we don't need you now."

A tremor went through Roebling's body, but with his jacket on and at the insistence of all of us in the hatch, he went up the ladder.

"Is he going to turn it in?" I asked.

"No, he'll go over and have a few beers and then he won't stay over so long," Roger said. "You know how these Yugoslavs are."

"He's not a Yugoslav; he's a Dutchman," I said.

"Yugoslav or Dutchman, he lives up on the Hill. All the people on the Hill, especially the foreign born, are scared of their jobs. Afraid the boss might catch them fucking off and can them. Roebling's no different," Roger said.

"Hey!" Someone shouting from above. "Is that ranger in this hatch? Hey, Borrego!"

"Yeah man, I'm down here. What you guys want?"

"Come up. We got a snake in hatch four on the second deck. Come on up. The guys quit working, the thing's long as a whip."

Another voice. "She-e-e-t man, hurry up. I ain't workin' no bananas with that motherfucker down there. Come up quick." The voice ordered Borrego as if he was the man in charge of snakes.

"Hey, you guys, can you handle it?" Borrego asked. "You better come with me, Joe."

Rapid voices, longshoremen's hands like fluttering birds.

"Calm down," Borrego said.

A few men still walked the stalks toward the scoops, ignoring the comatose and coiled snake. Most of the men stayed near and in back of Borrego, nervous and agitated.

"Hey, man, take it easy. This snake's not poisonous."

"Do the snake know dat?" a longshoreman asked, standing with his knees crouched, ready for flight.

"All the snake knows, it ended up on a banana tree down in Costa Rica, and it's heading for some glass cage in this cold-assed town."

"Do he know all dat?"

"He don't know shit," Borrego said. "But I'm going to take him out of here, so you little girls who are so scared of snakes can get back to work."

"Just get that motherfucker out of here."

I helped Borrego push some stalks away so the area around the snake was clear. The snake was a tannish gray color and had a checkered pattern.

"Is it poisonous?" I asked Borrego.

"No," Borrego said. "Can't always be so sure. It's not a viper, and if I could see the pupil of the eye I'd know for sure. Tropical snakes that are poisonous have a divided pupil. But new things happen every day. I'm going to grab the snake behind its head, and it will coil around my arm slowly, because it's stiff from the cold. Don't want it to bite anyway, as it feeds on rats and I might get an infection. I'll go up the ladder one rung at a time, and Joe, you go behind me and keep pushing me up."

Borrego made a pass at the men clustered near him. Quickly he waved the snake's head, and the man backed away.

"Poisonous or not, take that sonofabitch outa here."

Down on the dock I waited with Borrego. One of the gearmen had called the aquarium to come for the specimen. I puffed on a cigarette, and Borrego had the snake gripped behind its head with one hand and the rest of the snake coiled around his arm. His hand was slightly raised and away from his face.

A circle of faces, some men stopping on their way to the bars in back of the banana dock, others coming from the bars on their way back to the ship. Borrego talking in a monotone, relaxed.

"No, Charley, these snakes are born from eggs. They sit on their eggs and incubate them. But like you asked, some are born alive, especially the moccasins or rattlers down in Yucatan, but they're shorter than this and silvery. This is a boa constrictor, like a python, and it's not poisonous. Only problem, it doesn't like to eat dead things but likes chickens or pigeons or rats."

When the attendants from the aquarium came, they had only a flour sack—nothing as romantic as a cage—and Borrego drove his hand deep into the sack and released the snake.

"Hey, those guys in our hatch are going to be pissed. That truck from the aquarium took a long time," I said.

"Before we go back," Borrego said, "we'd better check on Roebling. He left way before we went for the snake. That's been over an hour."

I went into one of the two bars, and Borrego went into the other. No Roebling. On a hunch I went behind the bar to the extension of the pier where they had a couple of cable wheels that lay on their side, which longshoremen used for tables when the weather was nice. Roebling was there, seated on a bench but leaning forward, with his head on the table surface of the wheel, his white cap near the rail of the pier. Roebling's arms were out in front, over his head.

"Borrego!" I yelled.

When Borrego came around, we both approached the motionless Roebling.

"Something's wrong," I said. "He don't look right."

When I tried to touch Roebling on the shoulders, he slid from the bench, sprawled out with his head close to the stringer, his face pasty and gray and his arms haphazard above his head.

"Man, he sure don't look right," Borrego said.

I raised his head and the head lolled loose. Borrego took out his wallet and placed the celluloid-covered driver's license near Roebling's mouth. Roebling had quit breathing. I held Roebling's head. Borrego held his fingers on Roebling's heart and then leaned close and listened.

"He's dead."

"We better call an ambulance," I said. "Maybe there's still a chance."

"Take it easy," Borrego said. "He don't need an ambulance. I've been around dead people a lot, and this sure is a dead man."

Borrego reached under and touched Roebling near the crotch and in back between the legs. "He crapped his pants and there's some red. He hemorrhaged inside."

"What did he die from, that bang on the arm in the hatch?"

"Who knows, maybe shock, maybe a bad heart. There's no way

of knowing without an autopsy. But that ain't our bullshit."
Borrego had propped Roebling back onto the bench. "He's dead
for sure, and he's beginning to stink. We have to get him back on
the ship."

"The ship!" I said. "Call an ambulance."

"Roebling's got five kids," Borrego answered. "I met his wife at
a picnic one time. We're gonna do that family one last favor.
Daddy's gonna take care of his family for the last time. You have
to help me, Joe; he's too heavy for me to handle alone. We have to
get him back on the ship so his widow and kids can get the twenty-
five grand."

"I'm not sure we should do that," I said.

"Don't give me no ethical bullshit," Borrego said. "Fuck the
shipowners, those cold-fish uptown paper merchants been on our
backs for years, and this is one chance for us to get back. Roebling
spent a life working the docks, and he died on the docks, and his
widow deserves all she can get."

"Maybe she don't want it that way," I said.

"We don't have time for that. Roebling's dead, and he can't
make any decisions, so I'm making them for him."

I took off my cap and stood there looking at Roebling.

"I know you're not worrying about the shipowners," Borrego
said. "So it must be that Roman Catholic bullshit. We can't fuck
around here all day. We've got to rig some kind of commotion
so the supervision doesn't see us dragging him back. Run over to
the ship and get Roger and Nanakule."

Roger and Nanakule John started a commotion, a faked fight
with lots of pushing and raised voices. They were back at the
stern, and some men came to the rail of the ship, and others on the
dock stopped working the belts by the freight cars and trucks.
Puzzled looks on their faces. Not that two partners would end up
in a beef, but they knew Roger to be combatwise, and he'd go a
long way to keep from challenging the big Hawaiian.

I helped Borrego drag the dead Roebling down the dock. When
we got to the gangplank, Borrego just lifted Roebling in his arms
and carried him aboard.

"Hey, that sonofabitch is dead." Sam Brisket, the gang boss,
talking.

"You didn't see anything," I said.

"I didn't see anything, I don't know anything. I'm a blind man. Just tell me what to say about what happened below."

Borrego started to heave Roebling down the trunk that had the ladder and led to the decks below. "No man, I'm not going for that," I said. "Keep him intact. I'm tired of closed-coffin funerals."

"That's the easiest way. He was coming up the hatch and fell back. Hit the bottom, dead."

"No, that won't work anyway. Someone would hear a dead body falling down four flights, and he'd really be racked up. I think we should take him as far down as our deck and drop him the last ten feet. He won't be too banged up. You see," I said, "I know this is no tea party. But just for me, just for me, let's not mutilate the body. Just for me, Borrego. . . . I liked Roebling. I don't want to lay any phony lefty bullshit on you, but he's really our brother."

Brisket, the gang boss talking. "That sounds better to me. Fuck the PMA, but let's not fuck up the body."

"Okay, okay," Borrego said. "Since you're so worried about proprieties, Joe, you go down the ladder first, and I'll hang onto his jacket from above, 'cause I don't want any of that shit or blood down my neck."

I pushed back against Roebling's ass and hips as I skipped the rungs one at a time. Borrego had Roebling by the collar of his jacket, and with the jacket zipped tight, he lowered Roebling. When we were only eight rungs from the bottom, Borrego released Roebling, and the corpse and I fell into a heap at the bottom of the narrow and darkened passageway.

When we got back up to our own deck, I cupped both my hands and shouted, "Hey men, something happened to Roebling!"

Voices from below . . . "How we gonna get him outa here?"

"I'm rigging a sling," I said.

"Send him up in a pocket, and the guys on the dock can take care of him." One of the tricks of the holdmen was to put dead rats in the pockets and have them spill onto the line on the dock.

"We'll send you up in a pocket, and they'll take care of you!" I shouted to the men down below.

"Maybe he's not dead?"

"He's dead all right," I said. "Help me rig this sling, so we don't bang up the body more than is necessary. Oh, it's you, Sweetdick. Help me with the sling." I shouted up to Borrego and Nanakule John on deck. "Start hauling."

In starts and jerks, Roebling's corpse was eased up the narrow passageway. When I saw daylight, I followed. The ladder filled behind me with the men chattering, no longer silent. Not because they didn't care for Roebling. Most longshoremen had seen death enough times, but familiarity doesn't breed acceptance. I knew they would make a wide detour around death for fear it might touch them.

After the ambulance arrived and then the coroner's wagon, I pushed Borrego forward so he'd fend off most of the questions. Most of the longshoremen went on the dock, except the men from hatch three. We waited near the body, which we had covered with a tarp. One of Roebling's shoes stuck out. Across the channel, the windows of the telephone building were opened, and many heads popped out in response to the sirens. There was nothing to do, just stand there and wait. I tried not to think of Roebling. I didn't know what to think about. The randomness of life. Why not me instead of Roebling? When would my turn come?

The coroner's deputies came onto the ship. I turned my head and watched the debris in the channel as they shifted Roebling into a canvas sling. I watched them carry him off.

A man in a suit and white shirt, briefcase, a lawyer for the shipowners, cornered me, badgered me with questions.

"Wait a minute. I repeated that already," I said. "Yes, he fell down the hatch . . . How long ago? . . . I'm not sure, but he was discovered, I guess a half hour or so . . . Sign what?" His insistence on answers was getting me hot. My voice raised. "Man, I know you have to make a living, but I'm not signing nothing. Who the fuck are you anyway? Get your ass off the ship."

Sam Brisket edged between us. Steadily he pushed the man in the suit with the briefcase. "We don't sign nothing on the ship or the dock. The man is dead and that's enough. If anyone doubts what happened, there are hearings to go through. Why don't you move on?"

Sweetdick was at the rail. "What's the matter?" I said.

"I liked that old man," Sweetdick said. "That guy never talked 'bout what he was gonna do for someone, he just did it. Last week I got smashed and walked off the job, and he covered me. Some of those assholes wanted to call for a replacement, he vetoed it and worked for me. I got a full day's pay, and he never said nothing, didn't even want any extra dough for covering for me."

"Today, we worked for him." I put my arm around Sweetdick, and we went over toward the gangway. "It's easier this way. Zappo and it's over. Better than lying up in some hospital and getting a toe or leg amputated, bein' carved up a layer at a time. Roebling's in no pain."

"Hey, there's your brother," Sweetdick said.

Monte was on the dock. The administrator for the dead and the absent. He often said so himself. A Santa Claus business agent, bringing cigarettes and candy, bail bondsmen, pacifying the ship-owners and their lawyers, handling all the longshoremen just as he visited me in detox. The coroner's deputies had just loaded Roebling into their blue van. Monte talked in part to the deputies and to the superintendent and to the longshoremen: "I'm going to knock the ship off so there won't be any doubts today. Last week Tomaso was crushed at the steel dock in Richmond, and they took him out dead, but the gangs worked until lunchtime 'cause no one said he was dead for sure."

Monte would stop periodically as men rushed up to shake his hand. He always got a big vote and was a popular B.A. Monte prowling the ships for trouble. He consistently talked to the long-shoremen first and got their side. Then he'd talk to supervision. And he remembered everyone's name, greeting them. "Saw your Aunt Rose the other day, and she looks good since she's out of the hospital." Or, "Did your girl get into that school?" Or, "Man, your pop sure looks good since he's retired." Monte was old-time, but he didn't dress old-time. Today, a jaunty gray fedora and his fashion-plate suit. The good-looking face and the easy way of talking. He had the man with the briefcase in tow.

"Of course the men are upset. Honus Roebling's been on the docks thirty-five years. This is a well-liked union brother . . . Oh, sure, I'll fill you in on the details . . . Why not ride to the coroner's office with me?"

Turning to me. "See you later, and Pamela said to say hello."

He shook my hand and then Borrego's and faked a quick left hook at Nanakule that brought a smile to the Hawaiian's face.

"If bullshit was music," Borrego said, "your brother would be a brass band. Are you drinking, Joe?"

"I haven't had a drink in two months. It really racks me up."

"Why won't we go down to my spot and level out, get a bottle of gin and some tonic? God, I'm exhausted."

"Yeah, I guess we should say good-by to Roebling."

"We did the right thing, Joe."

"I know we did . . . I just didn't want him battered up. I've seen too many, so squashed up nobody could recognize them." I lit a cigarette and sucked on it deep. "Let's not get any Royal Gate gin. That stuff gives me nightmares."

After the third drink, the gin touched me. All the tension over Roebling, the snake, the screaming and yelling on the banana dock diffused as the gin spread through me with the same firebomb effect I always got from cheap tequila. We sat on a wooden bench, the gin and tonic and plastic bag of ice cubes in a big manila bag between us. I watched the ducks and the sea gulls faking it as ducks. Across the lagoon, the crumbling structures of the Palace of Fine Arts, the trees along the walkways, the darkening of evening. The drifting, easy caress of alcohol.

"How'd you ever become a ranger?" I asked.

"When I came from Montana, I found I couldn't live in a crowded, noisy city where people behaved like animals," Borrego said. "But when I went to a place in the mountains and the desert where it was quiet and peaceful with real animals, I found that I couldn't live there either."

"That's why you like this spot?" I said.

"I guess, but mainly it's an easy place to booze. No cops, and I hate bars, can't stand all that ragtime bullshit."

Some pigeons had come close to Borrego's feet. He scattered a sprinkling of crumbs. Bread crumbs from his lunch, I guess. Taking the Seagram's gin from the bag, he poured half a paper cup full and held it toward me. "Another hit?"

"Gin makes you thin," I said.

"Hey Joe, man, I'm sorry about getting you nervous about Roebling."

"Roebling's gone from my mind. If I lingered over that stuff, I'd be in the nuthouse. Give me a shot of tonic." I looked at the bottle. "We almost finished this fifth."

"Yeah . . . Look at those fucking sea gulls, coasting around, pretending they're ducks."

I poured another drink for myself. The bottle was empty.

Borrego stood up. "I'm gonna strangle a goose." He walked to the nearest bushes, stood with his back toward me. Turning around he buttoned his pants and walked to the trunk of the car. After a while, he came back with a fifth of Ballerina vodka. "Best I can do," he said.

"How come you took so long?" I said.

"I had the vodka stashed under some tools and the guns."

We drank in silence. People coming by, some singles and then lovers holding hands. I wondered . . . had Roebling been a good father? Had I ever been a good father? I tried to push the vision of my wife from my head. The big Portuguese wedding and one year later the birth of my girl. Thinking in that direction lay destruction. Maria had wanted to leave. Sever all ties, sever my relationship to my daughter. All this had been done while I was in a blackout. Not a literal blackout, but in a daze. Unable to make a decision other than to sign my blood away. My own blood, my own daughter. Maria Teresa down in one of the rice valley towns with my daughter, Rosalinda. For all I knew their names might be changed. . . The moon almost full. The dark of the shrubbery. The moon's reflection on the lagoon. The ducks barely visible. The entire area of the Palace of Fine Arts serene and peaceful. Inside me, the rush of something cold and distant. My inner discord . . . gray, lonesome, and despairing.

Borrego pointed to the moon. "You know, they're gonna shoot some asshole up there."

"Think of it romantically," I said.

"One more drink, then I have to head home to mama." He began to laugh. "You know how you always said . . . you liked thin women, reed thin."

"Yeah, slender."

"Sylvia's not slender. No, not by a long sight," Borrego said. "She's halfway between stout and fat."

"Don't let her throw a wrinkle on you."

"I want to feel something in bed. Not like you, Joe. The women that attract you look like they're one step from the sanitarium."

"The closer the bone, the sweeter the meat," I said. I wasn't thinking, barely listening, just reacting.

Borrego stood up and put all the bottles in the bag, indiscriminately, the empties and the partly filled bottles all jammed together. "See you tomorrow, brother."

I sat on the bench in the dusk watching the fog spread through the trees. In the distance the sound of foghorns. The chill in the air had come on sudden and quick. I walked up to my car and sat behind the wheel, smoking a cigarette, waiting for the car to warm up. Maybe tomorrow would be a better day.

I turned off Clement and parked the car behind the laundromat. Someone was standing in my doorway, and as I came closer . . . it was Sandy.

"Hey, kid. Glad to see you." I unlocked the door. "Come on up."

"I've been waiting here for five hours."

"You've been standing in that doorway for that long?"

"I went over to Miz Brown's for coffee twice, and I had an ice cream cone from across the street."

"Have you eaten supper yet?"

"No, I haven't, but that's not why I'm here. Remember when we were at Valencia detox and you said to drop by and that we were friends. Joe, I need a place to stay. I don't have a job, and I'm broke, and I have no place to stay. I've been staying around, and I can't stand to have anyone touch me anymore. I remembered that you said, anytime or always, there would be a place open for me . . . Joe did you mean it or do you even remember?"

"Let me come in out of the fog," I said. "We had a guy get killed on the docks today, and I'm half loaded. I do remember. Jesus Christ. There's no problem. You can stay as long as you want. There's a room in back, and I have extra blankets and even a sleeping bag." I took her by the elbow and led her to the room across from mine. "No one stays here. A Chinese guy owns this dump and the liquor store down below. Only other one here is another Chinese guy, young, a good guy, Johnny. We share the bathroom and the kitchen. You won't be any problem for him.

We're friends. Come on, quit worrying, you're home free . . .
I have some leftover spaghetti and meatballs in the fridge, and why
don't I go out and get us a bottle of wine . . . have you been
drinking?"

"No, not really, but I could stand a glass of wine."

Before I went down for the wine, I went back to my room and
took the rifle and put it in the closet.

We finished the spaghetti, and she had a glass of milk with her
meal. Then with the coffee she sipped some wine. We talked of the
days in the detox, of Arkie and Siberia Sam and the goofy teamster
with the mangy lion and the Warden, and how it was such a good
hideaway from the world and the police or the family or creditors
or whatever demons were in pursuit.

She was just as thin and just as neat with her Alice-in-
Wonderland hairdo that gave her that middle-class WASPy look.
The circles were still under her eyes. I asked her if she was on
dope, and she said no, not even pills. That she had a few short-
time jobs and that everyone was trying to get into her pants. I
didn't know if this was the truth or a way to keep me from hassling
her. I said she could stay as long as she wanted, and I would help
her out with a few bucks, and she could even use my car to look
for work. That Borrego could pick me up for work, or else I'd use
the 19 Polk bus that went right past the hall. That she was no
trouble for me and that I needed company, and she could go her
own way whenever she wanted. Most important, she had a place
to sleep and to eat and with no strings attached. I was tempted to
say that I thought of her as a daughter. For some reason I didn't
want to say that, and I didn't. She had the beginning of a few
tears, and we had another cup of coffee, and I put her to bed. She
had a big purse, a raincoat, a toothbrush, and not much else.

I tucked her under the covers. Gave her a light peck on the lips
and turned out her light. I told her to leave her door open as I was
just across the hall, and we left the light on in the hall all night.
That Johnny was a night worker and came home late but not to be
scared if she heard him in the kitchen. I'd have her go out and
make a key for the front door and for her room tomorrow. With
all that taken care of, I went into my room and threw my clothes
on a chair. I smoked my last cigarette in bed, listening to the street

noises and contemplating all the confusion of the day. The snake
incident . . . and like a perpetual movie that didn't stop, Roebling
spilling from the cable-wheel table onto the dock, again and again.
The way they carted him away. Like a chunk of meat in a canvas
sling, only the meat had a name, Honus Roebling. And in the
room across from mine, a bewildered girl. That's all she was,
hooker, pillhead, alki. A bewildered girl from the Golden West,
lost and adrift in the hard cruel world.

VI *Nymphets, Nuthouses, and Broken Booms*

Monte held Katherine's arm as they crossed the street. They had just come from the Curran Theater where they had seen a musical version of *Faust*. In the Theater Deli they went through the line quickly, then took their seats on the upper level in back beyond the potted palms.

"What a bloody bore," Katherine said.

"They try to be modern," Monte said. "All they end up doing is screwing up the story."

He ate a forkful of carrot cake and was taking a sip of coffee when his beeper came on.

"Excuse me," he said. He went into the lobby of the hotel next door and dialed from one of the phones. When he came back he put his hat on a chair and sipped his coffee again.

"What was it, darling?"

"A call from Sonoma State Hospital from a longshoreman. Told me I had to come up. They were making him load the pallets five high."

"Sounds like gibberish to me," Katherine said.

"It is gibberish. The pallets or boards on the waterfront are generally loaded three or four levels high for safety reasons so as not to overload the board. There are no boards up there. He's an inmate. Somehow he found a phone, and he called the B.A. number. I'm the night business agent this month."

"You're a bloody martyr for all those crazy blokes."

"I'm not a martyr," Monte said. He thought about it for a while. "I'm a utility to them. Someone to use and manipulate. They pay my wages, and it's more interesting than throwing sacks all day. Martyr. I never thought of it in that light. I guess I do more for them than most of the officials do. They're not nailing me to the cross, but they might be nailing me to the phone booth. In the last seven years, I've been on the phone more than during the previous forty-four. I'm a martyr phone junkie for every sonofabitch who has a complaint and a dime."

"Who is this bloke anyway?" Katherine asked.

"Carney. He's a perpetual shit disturber. Worked with my brother a few years ago. When Joe works, he's straight, but Carney's forever in trouble. Three months ago he got caught in a chimney. I hustled him a good lawyer, and he got a suspended sentence. Then he shot up the engine block of his own car. No police action on that. Last week he stuck up a San Francisco garbage truck and told them to drive him to Seattle. They got as far as Novato, flies hovering all over the highway. The highway patrol is sharp on the wrong garbage truck on the wrong freeway. He had the judge laughing. It might have been a kidnapping offense, but he got tired of holding the gun and gave it to one of the garbagemen. The highway patrol caught him right at that moment. He's crazy. The judge knew he's crazy. I know he's crazy. The only one who doesn't know he's crazy is Carney."

"He must be the most way-out longshoreman in the union?"

"We have others. Two years ago I had to go down to Disneyland. One of our gang bosses was drunk in the tourist submarine. The Duke of Cream Sherry. He was in the submarine with his family. Periscope up and torpedoes away. He had all the visitors intimidated. People from the Midwest out here on vacation are not used to this laidback behavior. I had to fly down to the Anaheim jail. But by the time I saw all those nuts in jail, the fire was gone. They're nervous little mice, wouldn't hurt a flea. I lecture them, counsel them, but it doesn't do any good."

"You *are* a bloody martyr," Katherine said.

"Maybe in certain ways I am. But there won't be much more of this crazy behavior. Handstow cargo is rapidly disappearing. We will soon ship more cargo with less men. This is the last gasp. Soon all the old-timers will be gone. The new longshoremen will be technicians handling sophisticated equipment. In San Francisco in ten years we will have a cadre of a thousand skilled men to handle the entire port. They'll be pinned down operating machinery. They won't have time to be wandering around drunk in make-believe submarines. Maybe that's why I put up with all this bullshit from Carney and from my brother and all his cronies. I had to tell someone, so I might as well tell you. Am I boring you?"

Katherine took a paper out of her purse. "I find it interesting. I can't follow all the technics, but I'm fascinated by your relationship to all these men and their troubles." She handed Monte the paper. "I hope you won't think of this as another assault on your time."

He took his time reading the letter. He took the cellophane off a cigar, sent a smoke ring toward the ceiling. "What does it mean?"

"Did you read it?"

"Yes, all of it. It's an offer for a job in Portland. Are you going to take it?"

"I just received the letter. I thought we should talk about it."

"A nurse can always get a job," Monte said. "There are other jobs right here in San Francisco. Certainly in the Bay Area. If you are dissatisfied at the convalescent home, then look around."

"Did you notice the pay! It's half again as much as I'm getting now."

"Why don't we think about this," Monte said.

As they were talking, a couple and a young girl seated themselves two tables away. Monte guessed them to be mother, father, and daughter. The girl was facing Monte. She had a wide-brimmed, white straw hat on the chair beside her. Monte judged her to be in her early teens, possibly thirteen. Wearing a white dress and white stockings that came just below her knees. She had short red hair in ringlets, and a few curls in front were sun bleached. Her eyelashes were exceptionally long. She watched him smoke, her eyes following the rings to the ceiling, a smile across her pouty mouth. Jokingly, Monte blew a smoke ring toward her. He expected her to stick her tongue out at him. Instead, she wiggled the toe of her shoe toward him. She did it in a manner her parents would not see. She continued staring at him, then gave him a sly wink.

"My god, she's flirting with you," Katherine said. She had followed the last few movements of the girl. "We ladies in our forties will have to barricade the castle. The bloody nerve of her, and only a tot. What do you Americans call them . . . nymphets? With that hair and those long eyelashes, she will be a nuisance. When I was her age, I was in knickers."

"Oh, she's just a young girl. She's experimenting. In safe company, too. If she was alone or with a girlfriend, she'd be a cool young lady. There'd be no winks or cute little kicks."

"Bosh. You were flirting, too, giving her the come-on." Katherine smiled, indicating she was not serious. But when she looked at the girl, the girl did stick her tongue out at Katherine. "What a treacherous little dear."

When they were in Katherine's place, Monte went to brush his teeth, to get rid of the tobacco taste and smell. For one second he did think of the young girl in the restaurant, but not in a personal way. That train of thought led to Joe. Joe favored young women, of course, but not as young as the girl in white. Maria Teresa had been only seventeen when he married her. And what of that sleek greyhound of a blonde from the detox?

Monte glanced in the mirror. Casually he scratched his chin, not sure if he needed a shave or not. He had always thought of himself as a cool guy. Was he such a cool guy, or was he a martyr, sacrificing himself for the longshore humanity? Monte tried to substantiate this grandiose image of himself. Justify himself. He knew a few longshoremen thought he had a water-repellent soul. But deep inside, Monte knew what most longshoremen expected of him. They didn't want him to be Jesus Christ. They didn't want him to be a duplicate of Harry Bridges. Their desires were simple. When they got into serious trouble, they expected him to pull the rabbit out of the hat.

"My honey, are you coming to bed?"

In the reflection of the mirror he saw Katherine waiting with a white slip on, carefully brushing her hair. One knee up on the bed as if she were ready to leap in. Her concern over that pouty and flirty young girl, calling her a nymphet. She'd be on her best behavior tonight, swing from the chandeliers if necessary. Katherine was too old to be a nymphet. She did have a shade of nymphomania, but not enough to get in the way of a good, normal relationship.

Monte walked across the lawn of Sonoma State Hospital. Carney had already been checked out, but Captain Coconut was a more serious problem. The lawn reminded Monte of the lawn at the New London Submarine Base. It had that soft, summery feel of Connecticut.

Captain Coconut was walking across the lawn with a child's pink plastic phone, a kid's toy with no cord. Coconut was talking on the phone, oblivious of Monte.

"Who you talking to?" Monte asked.

"God."

"Is that a long distance call?" Monte asked.

"No, local . . . Monte, are you come to get me out of here?"

"Einar," Monte, using his real name that many on the waterfront never knew or used, "I can't get you out of here, not just yet. They told me why you're here. Dancing around Myrtle with a butcher knife and her tied up in a chair. Einar . . . look at me, Einar. She's a pretty good woman. You guys been married thirty-five or forty years. I know you weren't going to kill her. It's not in you to be a murderer, but these people here, they don't know that, Einar. They think that kind of behavior is abnormal, a crazy old man letting off steam, dancing around his wife tied to a chair, threatening her with a knife."

Monte looked at the old longshoreman. The fire was gone, Einar's frail body, back braced against an oak tree, the plastic toy phone discarded on the lawn. "She has no one, Einar. She can't make it in life without you. I know stuff that they don't know. These people up here in the white coats, they don't know everything. On a scale of one to ten, Myrtle functions about two. You take care of her. She even sits in the car in front of the pier all day, and you eat lunch together. They don't know that you take care of her. Practically wash and bathe her, cook the meals. They have medical terms for your action. But I know you were just letting off steam. You're a man. You wouldn't tie her up to a chair and go through all that drama. You would have just killed her, just like that. Take her out of her misery. But you don't have that instinct, that flaw. I know you felt boxed in and wanted to call attention to yourself, to your predicament. Am I right, Einar?"

Einar was crying. The tough old Captain Coconut winch driver, who would deliberately sway the pontoons as he brought them aboard, bang them against the coaming. Tough gnarled old man, a Mission District longshoreman. Tough old man in tears. Thank God he hadn't accidentally killed Myrtle. Monte thought he understood Einar. This is where he had steered his life.

"Einar, I brought you a carton of cigarettes. These people took them away from me. I guess they'll parcel them out a pack at a time. But, Einar, they don't know. I brought you a pint of Old Crow, sipping whiskey. You may have to stash it outside. I didn't tell them about that." Monte gave him the bottle in a paper bag. He laid his hand on the old man's gray hair. "Einar, I know a tantrum takes two people."

That night Monte went to get Zack out of the Albany City Jail.

"Are you gonna get me out?" Zack asked.

"Yeah. I can get you out of any place but the cemetery."

Monte watched as Zack cleared the desk, taking the plastic bag with his belongings and signing the form. They walked into the cool night air.

"You know, I'm not your purely personal business agent."

"I don't know what that means," Zack said.

"It means, I'm not elected exclusively to be running around all the racetrack and fairground towns to be getting you out of jail."

"Naw, I didn't know that," Zack said. "What are you supposed to be doing?"

"Walking the docks," Monte said. "Checking jitney exhausts, faulty gears on ships, bent shackle pins, frozen blocks, overweight loads on the hurley gurley cranes, hazardous cargo. Making an appearance at weddings, wakes, and funerals. Visiting men in hospitals. Lying for men who run away to Reno. I'm at the beck and call of every sonofabitch who has a dime. I'm the walkng delegate who's expected to service and comfort all the men in the local, not just one crazy Russian who's buggy on horses and lives on Potrero Hill."

"I voted for you, Monte." Zack's voice trembled. He watched Monte carefully, emotional over his own statement. As if his vote for Monte explained and solved everything.

"Do you want a drink in Albany?" Monte asked.

"No."

"Why not?" Monte asked.

"I don't like Albany. How about the next town?"

"I don't like Berkeley," Monte said.

"How about Richmond?"

"I don't like Richmond."

"Oakland?"

"Yeah, we can stop in Oakland."

"Why Oakland?"

"Because I fell in love in Oakland one time."

"With a colored girl?"

"No, with a panda."

"What's a panda?"

"If you ask another question," Monte said, "I'll push you out of the car and leave your ass at Twelfth and Broadway."

"I'm keeping quiet."

"That's better . . . Zack, how come you're broke? Did those jailers make you for your money? Why don't you answer that question?"

"I had four winners 'n started drinking in the toilet with Reever. Treating the guys at the bar. I put all my money on the last race. On a horse called One-Eyed Gunner."

"He didn't win?"

"No, he didn't. He was in front, but the jockey fell off the horse in the stretch."

"Zack, did you ever think of jumping off the bridge?"

"I'm not answering any more questions."

"Just do that, Zack. Just do that."

Silence. Monte parked the car in front of the Twin Dragon Restaurant at Ninth and Broadway. Blinking neon lights.

"Why we stopping here?"

"Because I want some wonton soup," Monte said. "But first I want to explain a few home truths to you. One of the ways I keep sane is to avoid getting involved in other people's games. Particularly if the games are endless and don't accomplish anything. Zack, I've gone to my last jail to pick you up or to bail you out. I'm sick of racetracks and racing seasons and pissant city jails. Do you read me loud and clear?"

Silence.

Monte was on his way to the bridge approach when his beeper came on. He pulled his car over to the curb by the first telephone booth, in a dark industrial area of Oakland. Back into the car. "Zack, we're going over to the army base. They got a problem over there."

The ship was the *Gaviota Pass*, tied up at Pier Six. The rest of the army base looked like carnival time—lifts, trucks, freight cars, lights all over the four ships working at piers Seven and Eight. Only Pier Six was dark, just a few lights inside the shed. Monte knew that the army base had ordered sixty car-men today. A lot of car-men. And he knew they were loading cement and beer. What were they going to do? Get the Viet Cong drunk and then cover them with cement? He saw the crane frame of the Haviside barge on the starboard of the *Gaviota Pass*. That meant heavy stuff.

Lights at the gangway of the *Gaviota Pass*. Three men in business suits, two army officers, and an older Mexican woman holding the hand of a teenage girl.

Monte asked Zack, "Do you want to sit in the car or do you want to come along?" Zack stumbled out of the car.

The problem. The ship had been worked today. The Haviside barge with its big crane had loaded some army tanks into hatch four. A big Taylor lift inside the ship had pushed the tanks into the wings. In the afternoon they had shifted to the gear of the ship using the ship's winches to bring in the weapons carriers. On one load both booms carried away. Monte saw the wires and fall lines dangling. One boom lay across the dock. Unbelievably, no injuries, no deaths.

"Mister Karsten?" One of the army transportation officers pulled Monte aside. "This woman showed up half an hour ago. Her son is a member of the gang that worked this hatch."

"Yeah, it's Pistol Pete's gang. His name is Ultraza. Ramon Ultraza. He's steward of the gang and the only steady holdman." Monte had a picture of the boy in his head. He remembered that the young longshoreman was quiet, studious, and conscientious.

"Well, his mother said he always comes straight home from work. If he works overtime, he always calls so she can keep his dinner for later. Tonight he didn't come home. She called the gang boss. The gang boss thought he saw him after the accident, but he wasn't sure. One weapons carrier crashed in the center of the hatch. It's clear all around it. You can see that from the top of the hatch. Not only didn't he come home, he left his car in the parking lot. We checked the car. His mother had an extra key. We even checked the trunk."

"Dependable people don't always come home at night, and many times it has nothing to do with the job," Monte said. "Have the ship's electrician turn the lights on below." Monte knew this would not be enough. "Put in a cluster of drop lights. Zack, you go over to my car. Under the front seat on the passenger's side there's a flashlight. Don't get lost."

When Zack returned Monte went up the gangway, Zack behind him. The lights on Pier Six were all on. It was as bright as a night game at Candlestick. The army men lowered the drop lights into the hatch. From the deck, Monte still saw shadows. He stuck his flashlight into his belt, motioned to Zack. "Are you okay?"

"Yeah, I'm all right, Monte."

"Come down with me, and don't fall down the fucking hatch."

Monte went over the hatch one time. Nothing. He moved between and over the weapons carriers that had already been lashed. Then an idea. He decided to go over the hatch once more, slowly and carefully. He looked at the big Taylor forklift parked out of the square over in the wing. Monte recrossed the square of the hatch. On his knees, he flashed his light under and over the forklift. Jeeps, already lashed. He flashed his light inside each one. One jeep had a metal grating stuck into the canvas top. Red paint or blood on the grating. In the jeep behind the one that had the grating stuck in the top, in the back seat, sprawled out and hidden, Ramon Ultraza. Half his head torn away. Blood-covered face and neck. A hideous mangling. Monte glanced back to the deck. When the booms had collapsed, part of the grating and the frame where the winch driver stood carried away. How had the winch drivers managed to get clear of the flying booms and the grating? The disaster was limited to one man, Ultraza. Zack came over and looked at Ultraza.

"Should I go out to the square and call them down?"

"No, not yet." Monte reached in and put his finger on Ultraza's neck. The body was cold. "He's dead. I'll break it to his mother." Monte wiped blood from his hand. He took a small pad from his pocket. He drew a sketch of the hatch and all the vehicles, wrote down a concise history of what he thought had happened. He would check with Pistol Pete in the morning. He guessed that the boy had done everything right. Probably had been sitting on the forklift. He heard the booms go and scattered off the big forklift into the back of one of the jeeps. True, he may have been asleep in back of the jeep, but Monte doubted that. When the winch driver saw the booms go, perhaps—Monte could only guess—he shut off the juice and ran behind the stanchions that held the booms. When the booms snapped, they snapped the grating. A one out of a lifetime shot, the grating ricocheting into the hatch to find Ultraza.

The random finger of fate. Monte asked himself . . . Why didn't the good Lord, if there was a good Lord, select for extinction the fuckups, the drunks, the cheats, the lazies, and the liars? They died sure enough and sometimes before their time. But Ultraza? The boy supported his sister and his mother. Served the union as a steward. Worked hard as a holdman for his gang. Dead before he had a chance.

Monte did not bog down in this swamp of sentimentality. He thought about it. Measured it. Allowed this random of selection of a victim to disturb him. Disturb him for a short time. Then Monte covered it over with a coldness that was his own. Sentimentality was a trap, and that was not his game. He'd leave that to his brother Joe.

"Tough shot," Zack said. "Finding the kid like that."

"Yeah, and there's another tough shot," Monte said.

"What's that?"

"Going out and explaining his death to his mother."

VII   *The Girl of the Golden West*

Life changed for me when Sandy moved in. I was in the doldrums for years, trying to get Maria Teresa out of my system. But nothing seemed to work. I didn't attempt to find another woman, and I lost my interest in sports. I had always liked the track, and now I hardly ever watched the horses. Reno was always a drag for me, except whenever Borrego and I went hunting at Secret Pass in the Ruby Mountains. Then we'd hit Reno on the way back. The Russian River likewise. It had always been a good place to lie around during the days I was married—children splashing near the slides and families spread out on blankets eating picnic lunches. Now, too many memories for me.

Since I'd been on my own, all my fishing gear was gone, including the long rods for surf fishing and the trout rods and boots and raingear for the steelheads. Piece by piece everything disappeared, the Coleman lamps and all the rock-hounding equipment.

I recalled the secondhand Jeep with no top and my daughter so small I had to strap her into the seat whenever we went to Pigeon Point. How many years ago? Pigeon Point, where the old lighthouse dominated the point. Where we searched the rocks, splashing into the water for the sea anemones and sea urchins and all the marine life that hid in the coves. The search for whalebones on Whale Beach near Point Reyes.

The one time we went to Oildale, all of us, Maria Teresa and Rosalinda, my daughter. We watched the old buckets filled with nuts and bolts, which acted as counterweights for the oil pumps, and we found sharks' teeth on Sharkstooth Hill. My daughter laughing when I polished the tooth. Had someone at the San Francisco Gem and Mineral Society set it into a pendant with a gold chain, a necklace for her. Those days were gone. There was only one thing left in their place. John Barleycorn. Good old American booze and cheap wine.

Sandy changed all that. She had wiped Maria Teresa out of my system, and rarely did I think of my daughter. Sandy came into my life accidentally. I had assumed she would come out of the detox and end up as some high-class call girl. With each year I expected her to bounce down to a lower level and that I'd never see her again.

Never happened. She kept house for me the first week. We ate together and began to drink together. She liked Johnny, the young Chinese cook who lived in the back. He liked her and even made a big chop suey and fish dish for her. He never asked questions. That's not the Chinese style.

I lived in this flat above a liquor store because it had five bars within two blocks, and three of the bars opened at six in the morning. Sandy and I didn't visit these bars but concentrated our drinking at home, drinks centered around the meals by candlelight in the kitchen. Johnny and I sprayed the rooms with Black Flag to eliminate the cockroaches. I had a back-alley longshore mechanic tune up the car and put on new brake bands, so we could ride in safety.

Sandy, for some reason, seemed able to control her drinking. She liked wine better than hard liquor, but grew to like coffee royals in the mornings. We hardly ever got loaded, just tipsy and loose enough to relax with each other.

I was coming off a long desert of sexual inactivity. I hadn't slept with a so-called straight woman since Maria Teresa. On the trips to Nevada with Borrego, we hit the whorehouses at Mustang and the Moonlight Ranch. When Borrego married the trips ended.

Sandy loved the country and the outdoors. She and I drove up to the Sebastiani Winery in Sonoma. When we drove past the nut-house in Sonoma I thought of Captain Coconut. How he danced around his wife who was tied up in a chair, dancing around her with a big butcher knife. They locked him up tighter than a drum in the rubber room in the nuthouse. He was cuckoo, no doubt of that. I felt sorry for the old man. Even Monte couldn't get him out, and I'm not sure that was good idea, anyway.

All of the three wine valleys, Napa, Sonoma, and Mendocino, had nuthouses located in them. What was the meaning behind that?

After the winery, we went over a winding back road into the Napa Valley. We had lunch in a small state park off the road and finished two bottles of wine. At Calistoga we went swimming in a pool warmed by thermal springs. We dived under the water, and our strokes and love pats became more intimate and more sexual. We tried games. Each standing at the opposite side of the pool, then both of us swimming and meeting at the tile bottom, kissing as we met. Then arms circling each other, bubbles of air from our mouths as our lips stayed together and we kicked to the surface.

I joked with her. "When we came in I noticed all the swimmers and health nuts watching us. They're thinking . . . there's a nice old man with his lovely daughter."

"They know I'm not your daughter, and forty-five is not an old man. There's not a bit of gray in your hair, and I look older than I am. They could care less, worrying about their mudbaths and suntans and all their little health goodies. We should have another bottle of wine; then you would not be so self-conscious. I didn't want to tell you. I have a confession to make. Joe, I'm not twenty-eight. I'm only twenty-five. I looked so creepy and washed out in detox that I added a few years to my age. Don't pretend about age. We're only here for a day, and I'm your girl."

"Dive in again," I said. "Only this time we'll try to stay longer on the bottom." There's no fool like an old fool.

Afterward we walked around the town. We held hands for the first time. We decided to stay for supper and found a quiet restaurant. We had a couple of martinis and wine with our meal and some Drambuie after coffee. Outside, in the last dazzle of afternoon sun and hit by the soft warm air, we wandered between the trees.

Our kisses were getting deeper and longer. Tongues zipping in and out. Once we leaned against an oak tree, I kissed her so hard and squeezed her so tight that we were both out of breath.

"Joe, not so hard; you'll break my ribs. Not the kisses. Kiss me hard as you like. The strength in your arms. I'm not a sack of coffee. Don't get perturbed. Squeeze me hard as you like, bite me if you want too. God, we'll never get home."

I took her by the hand, and we walked toward the center of town. "I'm getting us a motel. First off, we go to the liquor store and pick up a bottle of gin."

Her body had very few scars, except along her backbone where she had had an operation for trouble with her back. She had a silken, smooth body for the type of life she had lived. She was evenly proportioned. She had small, firm breasts, with a big nipple in relation to the breast. All her skin was tight, with the muscles smooth, not bulky. She had the strong thighs that I like in a woman. The slight knock to her knees gave the legs a symmetrical look. The slender firm calves of her legs were not as muscular as the thighs. She held herself erect, her forehead coming even with my eyes. I already knew she was a trifle over five foot seven.

"How tall are you, Joe?"

"Just under six feet. I can make it by breathing deep and holding my head high, but not quite. Monte made it, but I didn't. He's an inch or two over."

"Bet he doesn't have those strong arms and those big hands I never noticed before. My but your fingers are long."

"It's from hard work. Maybe playing ball. Our dad was a miner, and he had big hands. Maybe we all picked that up."

All the shadows were gone from her eyes. My fingers locked in and massaged her short curly hair. "I love your hair," I said.

"I used to wear it down to my waist. My hair grows fast," she said. "I cut it for the first time when I worked on Sunset Boulevard. Long hair made me look too young, though it turned my customers on. The men wanted them younger and younger, teenyboppers if possible. But they always worried that we hippie gals didn't take baths."

She used no makeup, so her skin was clear. Her lips were full and her teeth white, even the one front tooth that had been chipped. A customer had hit her. A dentist put on a cap, but the cap got lost in the last stretch of drinking. When she kissed, she always closed her eyes.

Her hair on the mound at the juncture of her thighs was short, curly, and blonde. As we kissed our bodies twisted and turned. My mouth crushed those short and curly hairs, my tongue probing inside. Diving in the muff, tasting the pink and coral and almond flavors. Conscious of her tongue on my cock, teasingly up and down. I'd have come but for the booze. My attention divided. My mouth engulfing her, the sweet taste, the short hairs brushed flat against my teeth. Her mouth, with the interesting way of biting the sensitive areas, not hard, only a nibble. Then a suction that became strong. She moaned.

The thought came that she might be play acting, some girl-client style from the past. But the past was past. We were together. I had no complaints to have a young and tender woman. Young compared to me and even to Maria Teresa, who must be at least in her forties. Young compared to Pamela, who walked as if she had a corncob stuck up her ass. We were coming, and my juice mixed with her moans.

"Joe, you came all over my hair. Next time I'll hold him so close and get it all in my mouth. Do you like it that way?"

"Any way, any way," I said. We began kissing again.

I came two more times. The last time took so long and hard with us pounding the bed as I stroked her. She couldn't get the right punchback as the mattress was soft. We moved onto the floor, putting the blankets down with two pillows under her. I rode her as if she were a bronco and I was sunfishing. It seems corny, but it was sex and struggle and sweat and sperm and mouth spit as we rolled on and off the pillows. She tried to keep her ass on the pillows, bracing with her strong thighs, her youth giving me that pushback. None of that coy scariness. She had none of that. But with her athletic firmness, the pumping back and the rocking from side to side, zappo, I exploded for the third time. I didn't count the trembly shivers and eye-rolling times she came. We were so wiped out, so sweaty, with my heart pounding. She worried about that. I had bitten her on the thigh and on the lips, and I tasted blood while I manhandled her. She liked every minute of it. Fucking for me had never been so good.

"Ooh, ohhh, ohhh, Joe, that was so good. I came and came, hot as a firecracker. Shocks of electricity going through me, with all the magical precious feeling it ever had. Joe, when I saw you at Valencia, I knew you were a man. Those tireless arms. You're a regular octopus, a grizzled grizzly bear. Do you know what I am?"

"A puma. A pummeled puma. A mean-moving lithe . . . did I say that right? A lithe mean-moving puma who thinks she's a panther. A delicate-skinned fucking machine from a place where they breed fucking machines, the meadowlark state, the equality state, in old Wyoming."

"Joe, you remembered."

"You said you were born in Wyoming."

"That's what they called me when I first came to the Coast. That was my nickname among the hippie girls and later among the hookers. But since I've lived out here in all the big towns, I played that down." She mimicked a western drawl. "Came to the big towns looking for a man forsure, that's French, looking forsure for a French man. Not French in nationality, but . . ."

"I hate the French," I said. "But I love to French."

"That's getting into the thick of it, like the Indian maid said to Custer. Kiss me all over, Custer buster. Now that I found a forsure man, I'm not going to let him go. I'm gonna get us another job, and I'm gonna give him my best puma, slinky, slippery fucking machine action. If I catch him with another woman, I'll scratch her eyes from her head, forsure, and that's French. Joseph Karsten. Joey, the longshoreman. Yes, another job. I already applied for a job running a switchboard in a brokerage house. Brother, they don't know they're getting a Wyoming-born and puma-educated fucking machine. Only they aren't going to get the fucking part, only the typing and the perfect diction. All the puma fucking action is going to be reserved for a shorter-than-six-foot long-shoreman. A grizzly torsoed, octopus-armed longshoreman who really knows how to swim in warm water, serves high-class wine and petrifying gin that makes you thin. Knows how to make love and tickles and twirls the parts that makes a Wyoming girl come in flushes and gushes. I'm getting out of wind from talking. The puma done give out."

She fell back into my arms.

We lay on the floor with the blankets misshapen about us, our heads on a pillow. The funny bugs clicking outside, and the country smells of bougainvillea and night-blooming jasmine. From our vantage on the floor, we could see the sycamore trees with their big leaves and the eucalyptus at the back of the motel. Sandy and I lay there, our arms locked around each other. No heavy breathing or sweating, just holding each other tight. We smoked in the dark until it became chilly. Then I mixed us two big gins and tonic, and we went to sleep. No dreams, no thinking, no comparisons, and no worrying if this might end. Nothing but good feelings. I didn't dream or wish or hope or even feel exhausted. No Roebling, no falling booms, no chicken-shit divorce courts or banged-up cars or drug-free detox centers. Bump. I fell into a deep sleep.

Sandy took a job at a brokerage house, and she got on well with the brokers and the managers. Some of the girls were shitty because she made coffee when asked. They thought it was a putdown and that women are not chattels. They had a conference among themselves about Sandy making coffee for the men. Sandy told them to go fuck themselves, as they were middle class and had never gone without a meal. She needed the job, and it was her business if she wanted to make the coffee for the men. Besides, she noticed that the women also drank her morning coffee. She told me she'd hang onto the job. It was better than screwing every man who was dissatisfied with his wife and could come up with thirty dollars or whatever the hooker traffic called for at that particular time. Screwing was hard work unless one had a feeling for a man. She was blunt and up front with the way she handled her life.

Sandy put up brown curtains in her room. She put up new curtains in my room, blue curtains to match the color of my eyes, she said. She cleaned the kitchen and polished the stove. She mopped the floor, scrubbed the refrigerator to get rid of the sour smell, and disinfected the toilet. Put covers on both our beds, though we only used one bed at a time. Moved back and forth like a couple of vacationers. The entire flat began to have a woman's touch. We quit eating out. We were going to live like human beings, she said. She put ashtrays all over the flat. Bought me a modern Finnish reading lamp. It hung over the bed so I could read at night. The light came over my shoulder and hit the page. It was easier on my eyes. We had a new rug in the hall. Johnny was all smiles because he loved women and especially Sandy. When Sandy barbecued steaks he brought one of his many girlfriends from Chinatown.

She had this idea. That if we loved each other and didn't drink during the day, or by ourselves, we deserved a little treat at night. Maybe even a couple of bottles of good wine with a picnic on the weekends. She was good at omelettes and roasts, not too bad with Mexican and Italian dishes. She certainly fucked up her first attempt at a Japanese dish. I told her she didn't have enough seaweed in the teriyaki. She didn't think that too funny. One night she cooked a pork roast and stuffed it with apples and nuts. Mostly, she was good at hippie food with all the health ingredients. She admitted that cooking the meat was a concession to me.

I usually worked with Borrego. Whenever he took a day off, I switched over to Sweetdick. Sweetdick wanted to drink every day.

"We have this method," I explained. "Sandy and I don't drink during the day. When we come home at night, we eat and then drink later, have a few goodies."

"I think you're pussywhipped, Joe," Sweetdick said.

"And you're an alcoholic," I said.

"An alcoholic," he wheezed and hawed, "who's trying to call someone an alcoholic. Old wino, Joe. Who has his ass in gear trying to please some young pussy. But if one has to go, then that's not a bad way to go. Remember Blue Chevie Johnson. He had to go to the hospital to take a ball of hair from his stomach. That was from eating pussy of young gals. Cause I'm your friend, Joe, I'm passin' on this bit of news."

"Fuck you and the horse you rode in on," I told him.

Sandy had a four-day job. I started working Monday through Friday so we'd have the maximum time together. We went over to visit Borrego and Sylvia many times on their two-acre spread near Cotati. We played poker all night long, had salami and all-kinds-of-cheese sandwiches with all the stuff Sylvia had pickled. We played cards for a few hours and then started telling stories. We drank booze at first and then beer with the sandwiches. I noticed the women stuck together. If they had good cards, they barely bet against one another.

One night Sandy had a straight flush, and she really stuck it to us. As Sandy raked in the chips, she told Borrego, "You have the dead man's hand, aces and eights. Reason I know that is I'm related to Wild Bill Hickok, and he was part Cheyenne and that makes me part Cheyenne."

"That all sounds like bullshit to me," Borrego said. "Bill Hickok was part Sioux. I should know as I'm part Sioux. I believe you are, too. I pick up a resemblance to Sitting Bull in your features," Borrego told Sandy.

"Alvin, be kind," Sylvia said. That's the first time I ever heard her use Borrego's given name.

"Why should I be kind?" Borrego asked. "Sandy has not been kind. She made Joe and me pay through the horn to see her straight flush. Why do you women always stick together?"

"Alvin's just nervous cause a baby's on its way." She took Sandy's hand and held it to her belly. "Can you feel the baby kicking?"

One Sunday we invited Sweetdick and Siberia Sam to a picnic at McNear's Beach. What they wanted was a big booze bustout, and when that didn't happen, they carried off the day but weren't really satisfied. Happiness is the ability to find joy in someone else's joy. Nothing overt happened. Sweetdick and Siberia Sam were polite. They said they had a good time. They seemed to enjoy themselves, but I picked up bad vibes. They seemed to be together, and Sandy and I seemed to be together. Maybe I'm reading too much into it.

Though I was Catholic, we began to go to small, offbeat churches with a lot of singing and holding hands and making noise for Jesus. Sandy said that what she liked most about her hippie days was the sense of awe and communal feeling of religion and helping one another, like the Diggers. She still had those good feelings, though the dope and the hustles fucked up all the love. I said the funky clothes and the bags of food in the health food stores with all the people dipping their hands in the food and the grain all over the floor didn't draw me to their style of living. I didn't believe in sharing hepatitis. She said she didn't care for that part either.

When we came to a disagreement or a crisis, she never pushed, and I didn't, either. I told her how my mom said that if she ever argued with my father—and that was often—they always cleared up or resolved their differences before they went to sleep. They never went to sleep mad. Sandy thought we should follow the same sensible pattern. We even shook hands on it. But I knew it wouldn't mean a thing if the argument was big.

Monte said that I had it made with a sharp, foxy chick and a good cook besides. If she allowed me to drag her to the beaches and into the mountains and to Reno, I really had it made. He noticed I hadn't been drunk on the job since Sandy entered the picture. Both Monte and I knew old-timers who were general all-around fuckups. Then they would marry some Finnish or Swedish woman and suddenly they began to fly right. They came to work with clean clothes and began to put on weight from all the home cooking. They acquired a bank account and quit all the stupid borrowing. Behind a good man there was always a good woman. We agreed on that. I believe Monte was just saying that and that he was much more cynical than I was.

One Sunday while walking through Ghirardelli Square, Sandy and I ran into Monte and Pamela. Monte had on a beret.

"What kind of shit is this?" I asked.

"The beret makes him look very French," Sandy said. "Pamela has such good taste in buying it for him." By the sudden dark scowl on Pamela's face, Sandy knew she had committed a gaffe.

"Monte bought the beret on his own," Pamela said. "I hate berets. They remind me of men who carry pipes in their jackets and smell of garlic and onions and pipe smoke." As she spoke, her voice began to pick up venom.

Suddenly he knew that Katherine had given the beret to Monte.

Pamela and Sandy didn't hit it off. Sandy was too direct for Pamela, and Pamela was too wishy-washy for Sandy. She said that Pamela was neat looking enough to be a hooker, but that she'd have to get her ass out of low gear. That's why Monte was seeking his pleasure elsewhere. He wasn't getting enough at home. I asked if that was visible. She said that it stuck out all over. Monte went out and covered that weak part of his flank. She didn't understand why Monte didn't just leave Pamela. I said that he almost did, that he tore up all their credit cards and took her checkbook away.

Sandy reminded me that we didn't have credit cards, TV, or even a phone. That everyone had a phone. I told her that Albert Schweitzer didn't have a phone. She said that at least he had drums. We both needed a phone for work. As I was no longer persona non grata, didn't owe any money, and had no reason to seclude myself, we agreed that on Monday we'd get a phone.

The nights at home became better and better, as Sandy was not bashful in telling me what she liked sexually and at what tempo. She encouraged me to express my desires. We began to play games. She dressed in old hippie clothes or show-biz spangled costumes and sheer underclothes. We used all the spicy and teasing ways of handling ourselves. One night on the way home, I stopped off at Leavitt's and bought a gold ring.

I gave her a big kiss at the door. Slipped the ring on her finger.

"Why don't we try to build something together? Even make it legal if you want."

"We started as friends and you treated me gently enough to move us to a more loving level." She tried to stop the tears. "Joe, Joe, I accept the ring. Whatever you want. Making it legal means a home and everything." She seemed stumped for words. "I'd marry you. Yes, yes, yes."

VIII *The Eagle Cafe*

Joe . . . his brother. Although only six years younger than Monte, Monte thought of him as a son or sometimes as a child. A dreamer, unrealistic. A romantic, poetic man who lived in the wrong generation. Joe's vision of the world came from old Humphrey Bogart and William Holden movies. He was looking for heroes and justice and beauty; all he found were addicts, alcoholics, hookers, and a greedy, brutalized world he didn't understand. Perhaps that's why he always wore sunglasses when he was on a drinking run— to distort reality. Monte thought of him as an innocent who had fallen among evil companions. He never learned to handle booze, and he never learned to handle rejection. The constant mooning over a wife who had taken a hike, his unrealistic attitude toward his child. The dreaminess over their father's death, romanticizing the mine as a foreboding tomb.

Monte loved his brother, and each one of Joe's personality quirks taken alone was not severe, but put together they spelled trouble. He was literally stupid with women. Marry an ex-hooker? Sometimes Joe exasperated Monte. Monte understood that he himself manipulated people and cranked them up like toys, and often the toys went in the wrong direction. His guidance and manipulation of Joe rarely worked. He could never really grasp Joe. They loved each other, and it bothered Monte not to have some sort of control. Joe was controlled by sentimentality and a disastrous, romantic feeling toward women . . . and worst of all by an enemy who gave no quarter and took no prisoners—John Barleycorn.

Monte stood near the door of the Eagle Cafe. In the corner at two tables pushed together, Borrego, Sweetdick, and the rest of the gang were waiting for Joe to give him a send-off for his wedding. The bar was empty, only a few Muni drivers eating their lunches and pouring over the green sheet of the *Chronicle*. The cannery workers had gone back to work, and only Joe's gang was left in the corner and out of the way, waiting for him.

Monte watched his brother walk through the doorway, carefully stepping over a Great Dane laying half in and half outside the doorway. Joe walked up to the empty bar, not noticing the waiting group of longshoremen and not seeing Monte.

"Lou," Joe said, "give me a double gin and orange. Easy on the orange and not much ice." When he got it, he pushed the ice cube with his index finger.

Sweetdick came up and plunked himself down beside Joe.

"Give him a drink," Joe said to Lou.

"What's that, a guard dog?" Sweetdick asked.

"Yeah," Roger said as he came up to the bar and flanked Joe on the other side. "The dog's been trained to bite black asses."

"He can't bite me. I'm a Mason." Sweetdick flashed a Masonic ring on his left hand.

"That goddam ring's not gonna stop that dog. Where the hell did you get that ring?" Roger asked.

"I'm a pawnshop Mason," Sweetdick feigned seriousness. "That ring will stop a choo-choo train. Just flash that motherfucking ring, and the train will come to a dead stop. All the honky engineers kowtow to that ring."

"You stand on a railroad track and flash that ring and the locomotive will run over your black ass," Roger said.

"I'm not black, I'm a Portagee," Sweetdick said. "Give us three Portuguese a drink, Mister Lou."

Joe turned to face the door, leaning his back on the bar. By now Nanakule John, Borrego, and Siberia Sam came over, pulling up chairs and altering tables to be closer to Joe. Before the drinks that Sweetdick ordered came, Zack came to the table nearest Joe. "What are you guys drinking?"

Borrego Red said, "A vodka for Zack. What else?"

"I don't want a vodka," Zack said. He pronounced vodka as vooodkaa. "Just 'cause I'm a Russian, why do you always keep telling me that I want vodka. Give me a cognac."

"That's the way these guys are," Sweetdick said. "If they think you are one thing, they never let you change to something else.

Watch and see. They always try to pump me with gin. This is, except Joe. He never fucks with your inner or outer personality. He listens to exactly what you order."

Just like Sweetdick trying to upgrade Joe, Monte thought. And Joe always with a good word for Sweetdick. One time they drank through the middle of the Hunter's Point riot. Police cars scouting, people scurrying, even a few bad moments around the hiring hall . . . Sweetdick and Joe drinking together at Sweetdick's near Fillmore. Monte remembered that Siberia Sam had tried to level this to solidarity, where two union brothers of different races put their longshore brotherhood on the line. Sweetdick had said, "Sheet man, 'cause one bunch of motherfuckers want to burn the town down and another bunch of motherfuckers want to save their property and ass ain't got nothing to do with me and Joe." Joe had answered, "It ain't no big thing. The riot was into action for two days before Sweetdick and I knew it. We thought some wino had burned a couple of hotels. That's what the fire trucks and ambulances and police cars was all about. Don't make no big thing out of it. We're friends and we're not evaluating our friend-ship or changing our feelings every other day to satisfy someone else's political bullshit . . . gin is thicker than color. Ain't that right Sweetdick?" Monte recalled that Sweetdick had banged the open palms of his hands on his thighs.

Borrego Red watched Monte as he took off his coat and fedora. "Monte only pretends to listen," Borrego said.

"Give me a cognac, too," Sweetdick said.

"I don't want none of those fag knickknack drinks. Give me a double bourbon and a water back," Roger said.

"I want a Bloody Thursday," Nanakule said, changing the Mary to Thursday for the day that was a memorial for long-shoremen.

"Do you want all the garbage in it?" Borrego Red asked.

"Yeah, yeah," Nanakule said. "I got a hangover. Me and the old lady went to one of those naked nightclubs in North Beach last night. Skinny broads jumpin' up and down. When we get home, she sends the baby sitter home and turns on the radio. She get up on the kitchen table and begins dancing . . . 'n she's big, Hawaiian big . . . and the legs on the table are bending and the house shaking.

I told her, 'My God, momma, the people on the block gonna think it's an earthquake!' "

Borrego Red not even fazed. "You want all the garbage in the drink . . . okay, and you, Joe?"

"Gin and tonic."

"Double?"

"No, single. All these double orders," Joe said, "we'll all be plastered."

"Look who's talking. The biggest rummy on the docks," Roger said.

"Don't be talking about rummies. Our meeting is called to drink to a brother who's going down that old green river of heartache and despair. We've got to find Joe a sideline girlfriend," Borrego Red said.

"Every rat needs two holes," Sweetdick said.

"Where's Siberia Sam?" Joe asked.

"He's in the shithouse," Nanakule said.

"If you don't talk politics or union business, Sam vacates to the shithouse, every time," Joe said.

"Were you dreaming of the workers' paradise over in Russia?" Roger asked as Siberia Sam came out of the restroom.

"Fuck you, assholes," Siberia Sam said. "It's not all ham and eggs over there, but at least there's no boss breathing down your neck, no capitalist raking the cream off the top. No asshole driving around in a Cadillac smoking big cigars."

"Monte has a Cadillac and smokes cigars too," Roger said.

"Give me a break, fellows," Siberia Sam said. "I'm not into criticizing the American system today. I'm not even into exalting the Soviet Union. I'm here to have a few drinks and to kiss off Joe's freedom. I'm not criticizing Monte. He's not perfect, but he's one of the few business agents we've had who consistently comes aboard ship and listens to the workers present their side before he contacts supervision."

"What are you rinkydink shoe salesmen trying to do, put Sam and me on a collision course? I still remember over ten years ago Sam brought back a bottle of vodka from the Soviet Union for me. If there's one thing the Soviet Union produces, it's excellent vodka. Why not drop politics for today, allow the high mucky-mucks to take care of foreign policy. We working stiffs will take care of union conditions. Can I buy a drink?" Monte looked around. "I thought I saw the Duke of Cream Sherry with you guys. Where's the Duke?"

"I saw him leave before you guys came over," Joe said. "Maybe he went to a movie. Sometimes he gets his usual lemon cream pie and sherry and sits in the dark and slurps the pie and gets half loaded. He's buggy on foreign films and doesn't even understand the language."

Joe and Tony Priolo, two Sicilians who had a barber shop near the longshore hall for the last fifty years, came in and sat at the end of the bar. Lou went to serve them, and during the distraction Monte leaned over to Joe. "The world's more modern than when we were kids. Loads of people living together, not even getting married," Monte said.

"Monte, don't give me any lectures. I know you mean well, but I'm not into hearing any advice today."

"The East Coast is on strike right now. That's why we have all this work," Monte said. "Our contract is up in a few months. Everyone dissatisfied over the rapid mechanization. The union split over the steady-man issue. This is no time to get married."

"Everyone in a strike isn't single. People survived strikes being married," Joe said. "Sandy and I get along. We think we're in love, and that's enough for us. We're gonna try to build a life together. I'm getting married. It's as simple as that."

Monte shifted his concentration abruptly. He called to Lou, "Set up the house. Exclude Roger. I think he's had enough already." Monte reached over, ran his hands through Roger's hair. "Exclude Roger the Dodger, the old ratshooter."

"Monte, if I didn't know you any better, I'd say you were cracking up," Roger said. "Since you moved to Berkeley, you're going politico on us."

"I don't live in Berkeley," Monte said flatly. "If there's one class I don't trust, it's the middle class, and I distrust middle-class kids the most. It's fashionable to be radical and rant and rave for a few college years. Works up the blood and excites the girls, but ten

years from now those same kids will be working for some brokerage house or with their feet on some law office desk and their
name on the outside shingle. I hate Berkeley," Monte said.

"Send the minorities and the queers over to Berkeley," Roger
said.

"Don't shit disturb," Sweetdick said to Roger. "I'm a minority,
and I don't want to move over to that motherfucking town. And I
never sucked a dick in my life. So that takes care of that."

"Maybe *you* be in some shipowner's office with a shingle outside?" Nanakule said to Monte.

"John, I'll be doing business at the same old stand next year and
twenty years from now. I'm like the rest of the longshoremen. I
found a home."

"God bless our happy home," Siberia Sam said. "The next
drink's on me . . . and include Drugstore Hank."

Drugstore Hank had walked in the door. He was a longshoreman
in his early twenties who was a hype and an alki. He had kicked
heroin four times but never managed to stay clean. Heroin followed
by booze, that wild exhausting combination that gave his delicate,
fine features the cast of death. Monte considered him an airhead,
a space cowboy who walked three feet off the ground. Monte
might trust an alki, but he'd never trust a hype.

"Hail, hail, the gang's all here," Monte said as his buddy Eddie
Tijera came into the Eagle. Eddie, with his trimmed mustache and
sweatsuit as if he had been out rowing with the Dolphin Club—the
British commando image.

"I've been playing softball with the topless and bottomless
strippers team from the bar," Eddie said.

"I like baseball," Drugstore Hank said, "but lately the ball
hangs up there too long."

Two more rounds from Monte and another from Eddie Tijera.
The longshoremen locked into a repeated litany . . . endless rounds
of senseless jokes, senseless loading and reloading of ships, all the
women they had screwed, comparisons of the clubs in Reno,
which and what club had the biggest jackpots, what club served
the most free drinks. The fights in bars they had won. The fights in
bars they had lost. The cars they had totaled. How lousy the
International was—how it sold out the union. That Harry Bridges
had become senile. How lousy the local officials were, Monte

excluded. The existential ache and pain of everyday living that absorbed and somehow frightened each of them. Joe's good fortune in finding a young and shapely broad to marry.

And then the wedding farewell party broke up. Joe saluting the gang with his last drink as Monte watched him walk through the door, the bottle of Chivas Regal that Roger had stolen off a ship at Pier Nine clutched in his hand. Dangling from his work jacket, pinned to his back, a black painted condom and a small paper, clipped with a safety pin—Just Married and Pussywhipped.

ıx *A Short Dance in the Sun*

The day after the big blast they had for me at the Eagle, Borrego
and his wife, Sylvia, Sandy, and I drove to Reno. We were married
in the late afternoon by a justice of the peace, a rapid ceremony
with Borrego and his wife as witnesses. In the evening we celebrated
at Harrah's Club with champagne and a big dinner and Sammy
Davis, Jr. We all knew that I had been sleeping with Sandy prior to
the ceremony, that it was not as important for us to go to bed
soon after the wedding as it might be for ordinary newlyweds. So
we went back to the motel with bags of food and six packs of beer
and a bottle of Tanqueray gin. We continued our celebration by
playing poker until the sun came up.

Borrego and Sylvia drove back to the Bay Area. I asked Sandy if
she wanted to see Borrego's and my old haunt. I explained that
Borrego had been born in Montana but was raised in Nevada. She
was game. Without sleep we drove to Old Fort Churchill, an
army cavalry outpost that had been abandoned since the Civil
War. Nothing special, just a burial ground beside the Carson River
and an iron water pump with a sign that read Not Fit to Drink. A
few cottonwood trees. I didn't tell her the riverbed was a hangout
for snakes.

I took the guns I had borrowed from Borrego. Sandy and I went
to the cul-de-sac canyon where Borrego and I always lined up
cans and practiced shooting before deer season. I set up rusty
discarded beer cans and a few bottles in the canyon, varying the
distances. The morning sun gave the clay a tan, cakey color.
We were a long way from traffic. There was no noise, only the click
as I loaded the guns, a .38 Smith and Wesson and an old Harring-
ton and Richardson, a .22 that had a six-inch barrel and shot high
and to the right. Borrego had offered me his Magnum, but I knew
it was too heavy for Sandy. The noise and the shock of the kick
might frighten her. I wanted her to learn how to shoot. Not because
I worried about the creeps and wackos in the city. But I liked to go

outdoors, and I intended to take her with me. I also believed it was important for her to handle a gun. Lately the outdoors had as many creeps and prowlers as the city. There were always bears, and though I had never seen a mountain lion, I knew women had unjustified fears about them.

I had been a sharpshooter in the navy, and I plunked the cans one after the other. I showed her how to aim and how to squeeze the trigger evenly and slow, how to load and unload the pistols, how to hold her arm out steady and coordinate the arm, the eye, and the trigger. She hit a few cans and broke one bottle.

"How funny the world has become," she commented. "We have just been married. Instead of consummating our marriage in bed, we played poker all night, then finished up drinking gin and beer. Now we're shooting pistols. This indicates that cards and alcohol and violence has taken precedence over love."

"This is a part of love," I said. "I want you to be with me always. Whether I go fishing or to the beaches or to the mountains. I don't want you sitting home alone. I didn't marry you just for sex or to be a cook or a housekeeper. We're going to be buddies and mates and companions and lovers and friends and confidants. Sandy, I came to Nevada to marry you. This shooting at Fort Churchill is only an afterthought. I know it's different and might seem odd to most people."

"It's not odd for us to be together whenever we can. We should seek our pleasures together." She talked rapidly as if to cover her complaint. "I've been lonesome most of my life. Even lonesome when other people thought I was having fun. I love you, Joe. I know your life has not been a picnic. I know you never complain about my past, that you try to understand me. Some of the running around I've done might disturb other men. Joe, we're going to be in love forever and ever."

We put the guns away in the trunk of the car and drove back to the motel.

Sandy went to work every day and took no days off. For the first time in her life, she decided she wanted a home. I assumed we would just look for a bigger apartment nearby, someplace to live while we looked for a house. But after we checked the rents in a few places, we decided to stay put. I told Wing Tan, the owner, that she was not really my niece and that we had married. I asked him how much extra he wanted for both of us to stay there. Sandy paid half of the rent—that was our agreement. In a way it may have been confusing. It was as if we rented the entire flat, only we had Johnny as a boarder. I asked Johnny if it bothered him for Sandy to stay. He said no trouble, reminding me that he had not yet cooked a wedding dinner for us. And Sandy loved the easy transportation of the California and Clement Street buses. The increasing migration of Chinese to the Clement Street area added the name "Chinatown West" to the neighborhood. Sandy and I agreed, at certain times of the day the street resembled a flattened-out Hong Kong or Singapore without the jungle heat or the whiff of tropical flowers.

Although we liked the neighborhood I lived in, it was too expensive. We talked about our decision to buy a home. We wrote it out, paper and pencil, dollar by dollar. We needed a bankroll or at least enough savings to have the credit union give us the rest for a down payment.

"Joe, let's continue not drinking at all during the day," Sandy said. "I won't even have a beer or a glass of wine with my lunch or join the girls for birthday parties, like every other day. At night, we can have our party, just the two of us. Instead of drinking during the day, think of our future home and the game playing we can have at night."

"By games, do you mean Parcheesi or Monopoly or checkers or chess?"

"It will be an adult form of checkers," she said.

"You'll move, and I'll jump you."

"Something like that, but with all the gaudy variations that we can handle. There's a shop on Powell Street that sells sexy underwear for entertainers, loads of sheer, exciting, sensual clothing for women, and for men too."

"Stop, you're giving me a hard-on."

"While we're waiting for our home, we'll build a little fantasy dream house of our own," she said.

"Man o man, you must be rowdier than you look. I never knew you were such a hot number while you were spaced out on that couch in detox."

"Joe, I was sicker than a dog. You were so good to me, going for chocolate and orange juice and making me feel so safe and secure. Never making a pass at me. I thought, my god, this man is different. I appreciated all your generosity with money and with cigarettes. How the other residents respected you. How they waited for Monte to come and then have you pass out most of his cigarettes, gum, and candy. Most of all I liked the tenderness. Very few men have been tender to me. When I think of men, I think of an octopus with twelve hands and me fighting to keep the hands from running up my skirt. But you can be a big ole grizzly bear and maul me from one side to the other. When you kiss me all over, my toes point to the ceiling, and I feel I'm going to float away."

"I've been treading water for the last twelve years," I said. "I wanted to feel someone needed me. To have someone care for me and for me alone. The bleak landscape, coming home every night to four walls and a scapular. Spend the night reading the *Examiner* or else watch the cockroaches run across the mahogany of some jukebox bar. What good feelings to come home to someone I care for. I *do* care for you." I wrapped my arms around Sandy's shoulders and pulled her tight.

"I'll learn to shoot and to fish. But Joe, I don't want to shoot any deer. I don't want to look at those motherly eyes. It even bothers me to catch a fish. When it's flopping on the ground gasping for life, no one cares. People just drinking cans of beer and smoking or talking or casting into the river again while that poor fish is struggling for its life. And it's hateful to skin them, to cut its belly open and clean it out. That will be your job, Joe. I'll be the chef."

In the dark we held onto each other. We heard Johnny work his key into the front door and his feet coming up the long flight of steps.

Everything was beautiful. It had been only four or was it five months since I rode out the rip-snorting tremors at the detox. For years I had been on the same deadly circle. Drink sensibly for a month or two—or what I thought was reasonable or sensible— then the accelerated pickup. Drinking in the mornings, taking days off from work. Sit in bars morning, noon, and night, and then drinking solo in my room. Stiff senseless drinking, two to three quarts of vodka or gin every day. Shifting from ginger ale and Seven-Up to cream soda or root beer for chasers as I tried to get the booze down. I often needed a pint of white port before I started the real drinking. Then the ritual of covering the windows with black friction tape. The friction tape reminding me of death or coffins or my dad lost in the pitch-black mine. Hiding out and never leaving the house except for booze, and then scurrying back to my black hole. The wrap-up. Jails, hospitals, detox centers, and recovery houses.

Five or ten years ago, I could decide one morning that enough was enough. Sweat it out for one or two days on soup or liquids, then shake it out on the job. Wringing wet from pumping coffee or apples in a van, and I was home free. No more.

Now I knew that booze was not the basic problem. My former bleak landscape had become colorful, my life filled with good fortune. How random life was. How accidental. To find an agreeable and interesting woman, one who could ramble in bed. A companion who could cook and was drawn to a home. As a fringe benefit, those late-night shatterings.

We had different routines every night. She called them nightgames. Sometimes we had drinks before dinner. Tomorrow's preparations taken care of—house cleaned, possibly the clothes washed, showers taken. The telephone cut off or turned so low we couldn't hear the ring. No candlelight. Sandy said it was too middle class. More drinks. The drinks making our heads fuzzy and creating a general looseness. The jokey touches and love pats. Her knowledge of stimulation and turn-on. Her compact figure, even the scars on her back not visible in the turned-down lights. The streetlights through the blinds, carving our ceiling into zebra stripes. The aroma of perfume. Sandy always put some on the light bulbs. Sometimes we exhausted ourselves straight out, a pair of crawling zappy animals. I had bitten her so many times, she said, she'd end up an amputee. Most bites along her thighs and kissable belly. One night she came out of the shower naked except for gold Cuban heels that made her glide along because they had no straps. A red ribbon tied as a choker around her neck. I couldn't touch her for an hour. She circled me, playing with my hair, blowing in my ears, a slow teasing come-on.

Once she pretended she could not use her hands. She wore gloves and held her hands in her lap, and I fed her. It had a sensual effect. I suggested we do this in a high-class restaurant. She said, okay, but you wear the gloves. We were not into tying or spankings, as that disturbed me, but she said it was a turn-on for many older men. But she liked to be manhandled like cargo and to finish wildly clawing and sweating. That made her come time and time again. She thought of buying an exotic mynah bird, so we could have a jungle in our bedroom. We considered buying records of tom-toms for our record player or else records of old-time drummers like Zutty Singleton or Cozy Cole. We finally decided that props detracted from the pure blunt beauty of sex. We tried grass, but it made me sleepy. Sometimes it was a turn-on for her, and at other times she became slow and downbeat or too talky. It was risky to get me all steamed up and then have her talk of silly and nonsexual things.

In our explorations she found that I was excited by garter belts, long stockings, and high heels—especially when she didn't wear a brassiere or panties. She said that was very British. I said that I had never been to Britain or to Europe or even to the East Coast. If I learned any tricks, they were from Puson or Japan or Australia or Honolulu. We tried bathing together, but the tub was too small. We went out late at night for junk food and she wore a raincoat, only a raincoat. She had one that was very dressy from her Sunset Boulevard days. She'd wear the slick raincoat with nothing on underneath. No dress and no underwear, just the garter belt, the long stockings, and the high heels. My interest in this style of night dressing signified to her that my tastes were old-fashioned. On warm nights we'd walk along the Marina Green. Just the idea of her cool slim legs and smooth thighs and that naked ass under the raincoat drove me crazy.

We were in the new Hyatt Regency one night, half drunk on margaritas. We were sitting in their exotic atrium in deep leather chairs, with the inside elevators sliding up and down, listening to a piano and violin combo playing schmaltzy classical music. I knew she was bare except for the stockings. I asked her if we decided to screw in the lobby on one of the big couches, would we get away with it. We'd do it cool and not notice anyone watching us. She said to go ahead, that it would not shock anyone, as people were so brutalized from the Vietnam War and all the violence in the streets. If we did it slow and with style, they'd sit stunned. We'd finish and go off, and they'd wonder if they had a vision or had seen the real event. We were never brave enough to try it.

When we got home after having such thoughts and adventures, we kissed each other by the hour. From toe to head and back again, long drawn-out licky kisses. Our tongues licking as a cat might and then broader strokes as an artist stroking a canvas with a brush. The kisses along her inner thigh made her tickle and steam. And she had a deep and quick method of sucking cock, but that made me come too fast. We'd go from oral to straight and back to oral and straight again until she had a series of orgasms, and I had my one. We joked about my being the king and emperor and she the queen and puma cat, even jokingly calling each other Shorty and Lucy. But I didn't like those negative jokes, because they have a way of kicking back.

One night we went to see *Deep Throat*. She didn't want to go to some crummy Tenderloin or Skid Row theater, but we found that it was playing at the Presidio in my old neighborhood, which is really middle class and surrounded by bakeries and banks and no creeps. I told her to wear her raincoat that night, and we'd sit away from the men in their raincoats and we'd have a ball. She was already stimulated, as I had called her from work. When we got to the theater, the line was two blocks long with no men in raincoats. She held hers tight against the wind; she didn't want the totally middle-class crowd of dates to see her pillar and marble thighs. We stood in line behind two well-dressed Chinese couples. One woman even wore a mink coat. They were talking about their expensive orthodontist bills for their children's teeth.

The theater was crowded, and we were packed in on all sides. We only held hands. When we got in the car, I drove over near the pond where Borrego and I drank. In the shadow of the crumbling Palace of Fine Arts, I took her twice in the car.

I asked Sandy what she thought of the movie. She said Linda Lovelace made sucking cock seem like a lot of goddam hard work.

We tried every way to stimulate ourselves. We hiked to Muir Woods and made love alongside the path under the redwood trees. I'm forever turned on by the musty smells of the forest and the birds flitting around, especially if they're small and fancy colored.

Sandy said, "Your ex-wife must have educated you to this fancy fucking." I told her not to ride that horse on me. She agreed never to mention Maria Teresa again. Sandy tried not to rock the boat. If something worked for us, we tried it over and over again.

One time we were exploring each other, and she said she was not into anal, but if it interested me—and since we were in love— she'd not hold anything back. I told her it didn't interest me. We dropped that line of exploration once and for all. She bought some cookbooks, and we tried gourmet cooking and used some supposedly stimulating herbs without any special effect. One day one of the local pushers on the docks sold me on trying a Thai stick. It made me sleepy, just as pot did, but it made Sandy slow down and become supersensual and languorous. One week, after nightgames for four nights straight, I said that we'd better slow down or it might take the undertaker three days to wipe the smile off my face. She purred like a kitten.

There was a low-key side to our life, helped by a hundred nuances. We reaffirmed never to go to bed angry. We understood that all our problems were not to be solved in one day. We did not worry about personal freedom, that is, freedom to go our own way. We had been alone too long to worry over that. The security of our life was in working together.

She knew less about San Francisco than I did, so I acted as a guide. We took long walks in Golden Gate Park, as we were only five blocks away. I showed her a garden that was planted for blind people, with the names and descriptions of the plants and flowers in braille. The flowers and shrubs had strong aromas, so the blind might associate the smell with the description. We saw the bridge of the USS *San Francisco*, which had been battered during the war and was a symbol for all sailors.

I explained that I had served on a destroyer in the South Pacific during the Korean War and that this monument to the *San Francisco* had a sentimental attachment for me. And I told her about Slessor, one of my first partners on the docks, who had been on the *San Francisco* during all the battles around the Solomon Islands. A gray-haired handsome man, he married an attractive Scandinavian woman during the war. I visited their house often. They held hands in the kitchen and kissed many times and called each other Mama and Papa. Suddenly after twenty-six years of marriage, she threw him out of the house. He never said why. I thought of him as a good, hardworking husband who was conscientious. He had a few tattoos and chewed snuff occasionally, but never at home. Whammo. Out he went.

But what was surprising, he never mentioned her name again, good or bad. He came to work smiling and didn't change any of his habits. It was as if he had cut his wife's picture out of the family portrait, and no one ever mentioned the blank space. Most of us wail like banshees when we get eighty-sixed, reek with resentment and self-pity. I was unable to pick up any bad vibes from Slessor. At least nothing showed in his smile. About a year later Slessor invited me to his new place for lunch. There was a new mama there, a carbon copy of the other woman. Looked enough like her to be her sister, but she wasn't. Slessor kissed her a few times, and they called each other Mama and Papa. Then she served lunch. It was as if the past had no meaning.

I took her to different neighborhoods where I had lived, Glen Park and Noe Valley and the first place we lived after our dad died and mom came from Jackson. It was on Twentieth and Capp.

We always checked the real estate offices. In our slow way, we kept looking for a home. Often we hiked to Fort Point to watch the waves spray the rocks and to get a surreal shot of the Golden Gate Bridge from underneath. I liked the way Sandy dressed, hippie mixed with high style. She could alter her clothes; she came from the sticks and didn't have the do-it-for-me attitude of the big-city gals. She said it was better to buy good clothes and alter them than to buy cheesy stuff that fell apart. Sometimes she wore brown loafers and gray woolen socks over her sheer stockings, and with her hair short she didn't need a hat to protect her hair from the wind.

She looked like a college kid. One time I took her to the docks in Oakland, and she bought a pair of big sunglasses that made her look like a movie star in disguise. We ate at Jack London Square, and I had to tell her who Jack London was and how he was an alki, the same as we were. Before we went back to the city, I drove to Fourteenth Street near Fruitvale and showed her the large mural on the side of a wig shop. I explained that the mural was the vision of Mexico by a Mexican longshoreman named Zala, and how we worked together and drank together on the docks a few years ago, but that Zala usually worked on this side of the bay so we rarely saw each other.

Many times we just stayed home, and I read the sports page or we watched "Gunsmoke" on TV or private eye stories or cops and robbers thrillers. Often we went out to eat pizza or to have a hot fudge sundae. She liked to go to the movies and adored Woody Allen, but I said I was tired of all that New York neurotic Jewish bullshit. She asked what kind of films I liked. I told her *The Treasure of Sierra Madre* and *Stagecoach*. "*Stagecoach*! My mom liked that film," she said in exasperation. "I shoulda married your mom," I said.

We visited Borrego and Sylvia often and played poker. One time Borrego took Sandy out to the pen and showed her how to feed the pigs. That night we had pork roast and stuffing, and she whispered to me, "I'll never go out to that pigpen again." She was committed to visiting Monte and Pamela, but when Monte wasn't home or had to answer his beeper and leave, Pamela made her nervous.

Johnny was a joy to us. Often when we came home, he had dinner made. He broke the stereotype that says the Chinese are not expressive, because he rejoiced in our joy. Whenever Sandy cooked a big meal, there was an extra portion for Johnny. When Johnny's sister married in Chinatown, we were invited to the wedding. She was a tubby little girl, but Johnny's mother surprised us, a grand, attractive woman who moved between the tables and greeted people strongly and made rapid decisions, ordering waiters about and seating people. The wedding was in a small church where we had cake and champagne. Then everyone moved across the alley to dinner at the Canton Palace Restaurant. There were more than two hundred guests, fifteen separate dishes and a pint of Seagrams' Seven Crown at every table. Sandy wore a coral cocktail slip with a transparent black lace dress over it. She was the only blonde at the wedding and the only woman who did not wear makeup.

I asked Sandy if she wanted to visit her mother or tell her she had married. She said perhaps but she didn't know where her mother was. We called Santa Fe and Albuquerque. We also tried Denver and Cheyenne. We used all the names of Sandy's supposed father and stepfathers and even her mother's maiden name, with no result.

"Joe, if we have a home and we get our lives together, she'll smell it. She's like a bad penny. She'll come on with that teary, sobby you're my little girl and how she didn't know two husbands of hers were mauling me on the side. How she wasn't jealous of me. How I looked just as she did when she was young."

Sandy's face became grim as she spoke. "She'll say the men betrayed her. That I was her only love and she only wished she had the money to give us a down payment for our house." Sandy grew eloquent as she imitated her mother.

"Do you resemble your mom?"

"Not in the least," Sandy responded. "She put all her money on her back. She was a fancy dresser who was a sucker for college kids and beat my behind as if it was my fault if they showed an interest in me. One time we lived in Denver. My sister was convalescing in some home, and Mom and I went to Elitch Gardens, an amusement park. Mom went off with two younger guys, left me all alone. I was only seven at the time, and a policeman brought me home. Mother lied out of it. Said she had come back but couldn't find me. Of course I never moved from where I was told to wait.

"As small as I was, standing all alone in the amusement park, I made a decision. When I grew tall enough to pass for an adult, I'd leave her. And I did. I bided my time and withstood the pawings of uncles and so-called fathers, and when I was sixteen I took off for the Haight Ashbury. And all the massages and the hooking and the pills and the booze followed. I pray every day that I'm through with that part of my life," she said with a gasp. "That you and I will live happily, happily ever after."

"Amen," I said.

The days rolled by. I had never been so upbeat. My feelings for Sandy took precedence over any other feelings. Even my job became easier. No cargo was an effort. Borrego and I worked two days on barbed wire, a job that usually ended in skin cuts and ripped clothes and disaster, but we made it with flying colors.

When Borrego took a few days off to help his wife with the new baby, I worked with Sweetdick. Sweetdick wanted to josh and drink all day. I said, "No, man. I'm heading home to mama."

One day I went out alone to the steel dock at Ninth Avenue in Oakland. I didn't want to go, and while having coffee in the morning before driving over I almost asked for a replacement. But then I thought of Sandy and our future home and taking it one day at a time, and the job turned out to be a rumba. The sun shone all day. As I worked on the dock landing steel I saw all the ships sailing under the San Francisco–Oakland Bay Bridge heading for the Golden Gate and the open sea. Our lift driver, a Mexican old-timer, had just come back from a cruise. He and his wife had had a bang-up time, and he exalted the virtues and merits of marriage. Dave, the gang boss, had started on the docks in 1934 at the age of fourteen and had worked the docks on and off since. After the war he became a sparring partner for Max and Buddy Baer, and he played the stockmarket. Now that he was older, he ate health foods and had all kinds of home remedies. The three of us ate lunch together at a new restaurant across the freeway and the railroad tracks that offered all the chicken you could eat for a low price. They were trying to drag in customers. We gorged ourselves on chicken and had a mellow day of laughs and sunshine and camaraderie.

On weekends Sandy and I went house hunting. We started in the Marina district near Monte's home, but the prices had gone out of sight. The Marina home I had had with Maria Teresa had tripled in price, and very few homes were available. Even with the loan from the credit union, we didn't have the down payment. I had already used my California veteran's loan. The Richmond District was a desirable place for me, but there we were competing with the Chinese, who had bundles of cash. We even went as far north as Mill Valley and found a big rambling two-story house painted white over the wooden frame. It had a huge yard with two giant trees. In a way it had a Louisiana, a southern feeling. We tried to expand our credit with the credit union. But while we were running around like chickens with our heads chopped off, two other buyers showed up and settled the deal in fifteen minutes.

I took Sandy as far as Castro Valley in the East Bay. Castro

Valley had a big shopping center and better weather than San Francisco, and a few Portuguese longshoremen lived there. We calculated the additional money for the trips across the bay. Sandy didn't want to work in the East Bay, and I didn't want to join an East Bay gang and be separated from all my looney friends.

The Mission District had become all Latino, Polk Street was gay, and the area around Castro and Market was in the process of becoming gay. Looking for a home on limited funds was an education in sociology. I had never thought of who lived in what neighborhood and which ones were safe. When I was drinking all day and acting nutty with my longshore friends, we banged through the Tenderloin and even black bars in the Fillmore. Now, with a young and sharp, sexy wife, it was different. Sandy wasn't a fainting-lady type. She knew the numbers and how to play the game, but in reality she was still a little hippie-naive. She directed me to a big old Victorian two blocks up from Haight and cheaper than any we had seen. Her eyes glowed, but I said forget it.

We found it. On Army Street above the old part of Noe Valley in Saint Philip's parish we found an old wooden house. It was on a hill. Hard to park in front of the house, it was so steep, but a garage was under the house and an extra knotty-pine room was behind the garage. The house was one story but had a back yard with a high fence that cut off the visibility of neighbors. There were rose bushes and a stone birdbath. While we contemplated— standing in the yard, trying to compare the mortgages and the price—a butterfly flew onto Sandy's hand. She grabbed my hand and began dancing in a circle, and the sun shone on her face, bright and warm. I knew this area of the city was noted for its fog, but Sandy kept dancing and even pulled the real estate lady into the circle. Her smile and laughter became infectious. We both knew this was it.

"Joe, this is going to be our home. Isn't it grand? Please don't stop, Joe. We are having our dance in the sun. This will be my first and very own home in my life . . . our home, Joe."

I told the real estate lady we'd take it, and we went into the house to work out the formalities. There was only one catch. The owners who lived there were waiting for their new home to be finished and would not vacate for seven weeks.

In truth we were lucky. I came full circle. This had been my childhood neighborhood. All the pain and self-pity over Maria Teresa came to a dead stop. The dreary brutal drinking in cock-roachy urine-smelling bars was over. I pushed all this back into a recess in my mind.

"Joe, it's so beautiful today. The sun is shining and I feel like dancing in the park with my shoes off."

"Hippie style?"

"Yes, dear, hippie style. Barefoot in the grass with all the beads and bangles and flowers. Did you notice we already have two rose bushes? There's a whole patch on one side where we can grow tomatoes or zucchini."

"You're beginning to sound like a Yugoslav."

"Joe, tell me we're going to the park to dance with our shoes off. Dance in the grass with the sun shining so beautiful today and the city so white and reflecting the sun. Even the people are all beautiful."

We had lunch in Noe Valley on Twenty-Fourth Street. I bought her a bouquet of roses and went back and bought one red and one white carnation. The red flowers complemented her hair. We drove to Golden Gate Park to the hill by the glass-covered horticultural building—the big spread-out lawn. We took off our shoes. She peeled off her stockings, and I rolled up my pants. We began our dance. She did some ballet and then we danced the Charleston and the lindy and the Balboa. We bumped each other and hugged and kissed in between, then did a running splashy tango down the hill. We danced back to the top scattering the roses. She held one carnation in her teeth as we rolled down the hill on the grass, our bodies locked together turning over and over. The wind came up at three o'clock, and the fog perched above the trees. The after-work traffic was just entering the park. We put on our shoes, and I wrapped my arms around her. We walked toward our car.

In the shadows of the trees I saw tears on her cheeks. When I turned to kiss the tears away, her body stiffened. Then I watched her face turn hard and gray, as if a dark cloud had passed through her.

"Joe . . . I'm afraid something will happen between us and break us up. Promise me, Joe, don't let anything come between us.

If it happens and breaks us up, it will wreck our whole lives. We live for each other."

"Not everybody gets a second chance," I said. "But this is ours. We need each other and our love is too strong. Nothing can happen to us."

x *Election Day*

Nanakule John had a stroke. When Monte heard it in the morning, he called Kaiser to confirm the report. Nanakule was in intensive care, and his condition was critical. Why Nanakule John? Monte wondered. The big Hawaiian may have been a little overweight, but he was in good condition from good moves and from working every day. Unlike most of the hungry longshoremen who worked seven days a week, he took off on the weekends. He exercised with weights, but the stroke occurred in bed late at night, and now life changed for the big Hawaiian. Fate moved in odd and unpredictable ways. Nanakule John impressed everyone as indestructible. Now Big John was in the hospital, immobilized. Ordinarily Monte might understand if Joe or Sweetdick had a stroke or a heart attack, with the way they handled their lives—Joe drinking himself into oblivion and never eating when he drank. And he had high blood pressure anyway. Sweetdick not only drinking one or two quarts a day but up all night chasing women and screwing into the morning hours and coming to work every day without sleep or with little sleep.

This was election day, and Monte stood outside the union hall with all the other candidates. Merle stood right by the door passing out his cards. Monte didn't worry about Merle. Monte knew he was the front runner for president.

His opponent, the black and talented but cautious Merle. Merle did not have as much juice with the old-timers and the renegade drinkers. It was generally predicted that Monte would win and that Merle's time was still to come.

Monte had never lost an election for whatever office, and his reputation as a business agent was top drawer. All the loans he had out. The picnics and christenings, weddings and funerals he had attended. The trips to the hospitals and jails, many times driving the men home after he got them out on bail. Helping them fix their cars. Getting lawyers for their cases against the PMA.

His success with the rat beef. This was the day he picked up his markers. The irony if he lost by one vote. Monte was not mean—he truly worried about the big Hawaiian.

The light rain splattered Monte's raincoat. Under the new rules candidates could not pass out their cards inside the hall, although their posters hung all over the inside walls. Some had even tried to put their names on decals and paste them to the voting machines, but that was discouraged. Their posters were on the sides of the piers or in the toilets—their graffiti or their friends' graffiti or the graffiti they had written about their opponents written in chalk. The big paint job advertising REMEMBER CHARLIE. As each member came by, Monte said, "Give me a vote." He gave them his card, a simply printed card the same as his posters: A Twenty-Four Hour a Day President—Honest. Hard Working. Available. Monte Karsten. He talked to the young, the old-timers, and the loners, even men he knew were in the other camp. He talked to all races and all religions and all political persuasions. Monte took no chances. He had seen times when a candidate won by one vote and many times by differences of only six or nine votes. No one was bypassed. As each longshoreman came by, he gave him his short pitch and his card.

There were handshakes and claps on the back. Monte's personal approach: "How's the wife and the family? Tell your wife the spread she put out for the union picnic has me full to this day." Health and family, deaths and weddings, children and personal problems. Monte played them like a violin. In truth he did care, but he also had a bigger care in winning. The confidence that he should win. The acceptance within himself that he had done his homework. He wasn't here at the last minute begging for votes. His attitude was inflexible—I work for you three hundred and sixty-five days a year. Now I want you to go into that voting booth and work for me, for one second or however long it takes to pull the lever marked Monte Karsten.

Some of the men went in, voted, and left the hall. Others slunk in afraid not to take a card, so they took everyone's card and disappeared. Others were partisan. They went in and voted and then passed out cards for their friends. Others stayed around the hall and drank as if it was a special day.

Monte caught all his regulars. He didn't have to give any of his cards to Joe's gang. Roger came by and shook Monte's hand, nodded his head, and said he was going to the hospital to catch up on the latest about Nanakule John. Joe came by, and he had on sunglasses, the Southern sheriff kind, the ones he can see out of but no one can see in. A big smile. That hippie Hollywood broad had him on cloud nine. She must be a blowtorch in bed. Monte had seen it happen before, but he thought Joe smarter than to marry a woman so much younger than himself and with such a shaky background. Advice, however well given, was seldom taken. Joe had taken his lumps before. Maria Teresa and now Sandy. Where did he get these young bellringers? Certainly not in the bars where he hung out.

"Joe, did you hear about Nanakule?"

"No, nothing. What's wrong?"

"He's in the hospital with a stroke."

"That's why Roger came in, voted, and breezed out. Sorry to hear that. Jesus, the big Hawaiian. He exercised with the barbells and did yoga, and he didn't drink or smoke. You never know. I'll go and see him."

"I don't think you can see him. Only the family . . . excuse me, Joe . . . Andy Adams, you are a sight for sore eyes. See what hapens when an old friend takes a steady job at Fourteenth Street. I never get to see his smiling face." Monte extended his card.

The short, paunchy union member pushed it aside. "I'm punching the Karsten lever. These Johnny-come-latelys. Half of them work like fruits and wear long hair, or else they're shines. I know which side I'm on," Adams said.

"Spyrson . . . you never get any older. Look the same as you did twenty years ago." Monte gave his card to a gray-haired man who walked with a limp.

"I'm on a diet of saltwater and sweet pussy," Spyrson said.

A chilling wind came up, and many of the candidates sat in their cars or went for a drink or had their friends spell them and pass out their cards. Monte had Eddie Tijera working at the other door, across from the motel. But Monte stayed as the ranks thinned and it became dark, with only the lights from inside the hall to light up the small walkway.

Monte went into the hall occasionally to relieve himself. Periodically, he had some friend bring him a Styrofoam cup of coffee. But when friends offered him a drink, he'd say no. "Not yet, Rudi. But it may be champagne tonight."

Monte crossed the walkway to give cards to Don, an ex-marine who had fought at Iwo Jima. He gave cards to Nick and Bob, Bicycle Larry and Ortiz, Ramero and Wing, Badfoot Blair and Grover, a former miner from Nevada. Then he caught Broadway Eddie, a young Mexican longshoreman from the Mission District who was becoming politically involved. Eddie was already on the Stewards Council and was running for the Executive Board.

When Monte came back to Rudi Garcia, who had just offered him a drink, Rudi was laughing. "Monte, you're a front-running lead-pipe cinch. If you didn't pass out a single card, you'd win. This is your year."

Besides Monte's own style, he had a bit of the professor in him. Although he had only two years of college, he took this chore of soliciting votes and meeting new members as a challenge. It was a chance to perform his democratic duty, to present his knowledge of the job he was seeking and to show disinterested members the importance of their one vote—what it meant to the union and their families. If he changed only one or two minds, he had to give it his level best try, even if he was beaten. To win without arrogance . . . easy enough. To lose without alibis. He didn't want to have any alibis, at least not to himself.

He waited in the shivering wind. Close to closing time and he was the only one in the parking lot, the only candidate. A car circling, trying to find a parking place. He knew these members might not see him in the dim light, so he went toward the car and gave out his cards.

The polls closed. He sat for one moment on the bench alone in the dark, the wind bitter on his wrists, his body drained of energy. He lit part of an old cigar that he had jammed in his pocket. The cigar was crooked, and one leaf was loose. He wet the leaf to keep the cigar intact, took a few quick draws. He anticipated going in and doing a rapid rundown of the numbers on the backs of the machines, so he'd know if he beat Merle before the legitimate count by the city hall professionals who waited inside the office.

Sweet victory. The entire focus of his feelings and his nerves and his heart. And if he had a soul, it was certainly a soul massage. A confirmation of all his actions and the fulfillment of his goal. He wanted to be president. He worked hard to be president. Now the goal was achieved. Monte hadn't allowed himself the luxury of guessing or thinking beyond this goal. He knew it wasn't the end of the line. Constant vigilance and hard work would move him to his next goal.

Leaning back in his chair in the B.A.'s office, smoking a dark Honduran cigar, he accepted the handshakes and sometimes the drunken mauling of the longshoremen.

"It's the International next . . . right, Monte?" Siberia Sam talking. "You won three to two. Merle didn't even get a solid black vote. The boys in the International must be shaking in their boots. They don't want an honest man coming after their jobs." Siberia Sam held up his glass of champagne. This was the first time champagne was on the menu for victory. For years past it was mostly vodka or bourbon, but Monte had bought five cases of champagne, five boxes of cigars, and cartons of cigarettes. The longshoremen helped themselves.

"Right now, Sam, I'm honest," Monte said. "I haven't taken one red cent that didn't belong to me. Tonight, Sam, you are talking to an honest man. You never know what tomorrow will bring. The higher a person goes, perhaps—and I only say perhaps—honesty may become a self-defeating trait."

Sam's eyes became downcast. Monte reached over to touch his arm. "Sam, between you and me, if I ever go on the take, I'll make it a point to tell you. Not before witnesses or from who or where. But I'll confess to you so you won't have to exert your conscience."

"Monte, do you hate the old man?" Sam asked.

"No, in some ways I respect him. He beat Uncle Sam twice. He's financially completely honest, and he never used goons on us. He could have when he was really topdog. He always relied on his powers of verbal persuasion. Like he said, even his worst enemies don't take him for a fool. And I'm not his enemy—I'm a competitor. What bothers me is that he stayed past the last dance. He's on a power trip."

"I don't think you're talking about Bridges," Sam said. "Maybe you're looking at your own reflection in the mirror."

The news from the hospital was worse. Nanakule John was in bad straits. His left arm was immobilized, and his speech was impeded. Whether it was temporary or permanent damage, no one at Kaiser could say. His condition shifted by the hour. At this late hour he was resting comfortably. When Nanakule's sister passed a message from Roger to John, she said that John smiled. That was enough for Roger.

Roger wandered through the offices drinking champagne or a combination of brandy and champagne that he called a cannonade.

"That big Hawaiian asshole will be pumping cargo before the year's out." Roger's words had no force or humor. Roger's eyes had no belief.

Sweetdick brought a woman to the celebration, a light brown woman slightly older than Sweetdick and even bigger than he. She was well put together. Sweetdick had a glass of champagne in one hand, his other hand caressing her. Monte had seen Sweetdick go through some forty women. When he introduced the woman to Monte as his wife, it had no meaning.

"There's a call for you, Monte."

Monte took the call in the main office. Papers all over the floor like the end of a ticker-tape parade. Men sitting on the desks. The office girls with champagne, and more longshoremen drinking hard booze. Some of the victors, and losers, too, spanned out to the bars in the Fisherman's Wharf area adjacent to the hiring hall.

"Monte talking."

"It's Katherine. Are you coming over? I know when you called before you said that you had to stay around to celebrate. Are they excited that you won?"

"Most of them are wired from drinking. When we post the results tomorrow, the entire membership will know. I'm happy and glad it's over. I'm sorry I didn't call back. But I did call as soon as I had the results. I haven't even called home."

"I have a little celebration for us," Katherine said. "I made a salmon salad. I know how you adore salmon. There's some whiskey still here from the weekend."

"They're going through the champagne as fast as I uncork it. But there will be some left, and I'll be sure my baby has a taste."

"When?" she asked.

"An hour or so. In a way this is not only my night, it's the union's night. They selected me. Don't worry. I'll be over. Love you, dear."

Monte arrived at Katherine's apartment at two in the morning. She sat, hands folded, at the table loaded with goodies and plates set for the both of them. Monte had bottles of champagne under each arm. He was tired, and she knew he was tired, so she waited until he ate some salmon salad and a roast beef sandwich with a bottle of beer from the refrigerator.

Katherine's syrupy voice, "My darling, I know you are exhausted, but I think we must talk as it cannot go on this way."

"What way?" Monte asked.

"Don't play ducky with me. Didn't we agree after a few months to take more than a glance at our," she dragged it out, "sit-u-a-tion."

"We said we'd have a good time. No one would rock the boat," Monte said.

"But, darling, that was ever so long ago."

"Doesn't seem so long ago to me."

"Darling, my honey, times have changed. We met eons and ages ago. I have a chance to go to work at a hospital in Portland for a commanding raise. We should decide our direction . . . not tonight, as I know you are under wraps, but soon?"

"Decide what?" Monte asked. In truth he was not conscious of the direction of her conversation. Too much had happened today — the big Hawaiian and his stroke, his own victory. Now Katherine badgering him for some drunken promise while he was under the weather or in the heat of passion. Her infallible British memory. He was fuzzy and not enough in control to be argumentative. "Can't we wait for the weekend? I'll get away for the entire afternoon, and we can talk it over exhaustively."

"We have talked it over exhaustively . . . Are you in love with Pamela?"

"No, my dear, I am not. I don't love her. At least not in the way I love you. She's a habit, but, remember, also a mother."

"But the boy is in the university. A ducky boy he is from his photographs, but he is away from home and in most ways . . . I do say, on his own."

"Katherine, why don't you let things be for tonight. We can discuss it in the morning."

"There's never any morning with you. When the beeper comes on, off you go. We have failed to resolve this for the last three weeks. Remember, I brought it up as soon as I heard of the offer."

By now Monte's head began to clear. He was not stone cold drunk, but all the champagne and excitement had him in cold storage. He came up for air and took a good look at Katherine, her thin face and coppery red hair, the green eyes and the immaculate apartment, the perennial teapot. She had a few lines in her face, but didn't everyone. She was so much more a woman than Pamela.

He envisioned the drag of a breakup with Pamela. The boy and a sticky divorce, the community property and the hassling in court. He had gone through it so many times with other longshoremen, and they always got the short end of the stick. Now he was their president, but he knew the longshoremen understood human frailty. Besides, all the runners and shooters and swingers were divorced.

An idea crossed his mind. It was not a dream or a fantasy. The Coast Committee was in trouble. They needed new blood. His eyes scanned the mythical landscape. He had a strong vote and powerful union friends in the Seattle and Los Angeles locals. Who was in a stronger position to move to the International level and be a member of the all-powerful, three-man Coast Committee? A divorce? Bridges would not take him lightly, didn't want him near the top. Harry would lay the boobytraps, and Monte knew he'd have to defuse and negate all the traps. No matter how much energy he had, he couldn't scatter it to the wind. Not even for a slim and many times delightful English lady. Monte admitted that she was a lady and attractive, but with an attractiveness that showed the lines of age. He also suspected her feisty, aggressive manner might be troublesome in the long haul. Pamela was a cakewalk to handle. Just give her a credit card, and she'd be satisfied. Monte was capable of saying, "Fuck you, do what you want to do." Capable of wiping a woman from his life and not even thinking of it again. Not like Joe, who became dreamy and misguided.

"I have a three-week period to accept the position."

"I will make a decision by then. It will be a solid decision." He had already made the decision. Not to make a decision is a decision.

Women were a puzzle. He distinctly remembered that Katherine had gone along with the game plan. She understood that a divorce was not an option. That they'd have an affair or call it being in love, that their love transcended marriage and divorce. She was never left brooding all alone. He was smart enough not to keep her hidden, smart enough to introduce her to his friends. He just kept her clear of Pamela. Joe and Sandy saw them walking along the waterway in Sausalito. The four of them had coffee and chocolate together. She called frequently, and the girls in the office knew her by name and put her right through. No, Katherine was not isolated and actually had more bedtime with him than Pamela did. Why add additional problems for himself? Besides, he did not want to live with Katherine and the oath forever and forever. He had moved beyond the love of women. They were necessary to satisfy an itch, but once the itch was satisfied, Monte had trouble concentrating on them. It was hard to keep his feet from moving on. His mind was not on sex or love, but on his victory and the positioning for a possible future with the Coast Committee.

But he knew he had to come at least once, maybe twice more, as Katherine was a minx in bed.

Monte finished moving into the large paneled office of the presidency of Local 10. The move took a short time, as Monte did not like a cluttered office or desk. He put one suit, a sport jacket, a few shirts, two ties, and an extra hat, a Borsalino, into the closet. A few magazines into a drawer. He called them catch-up magazines. *U.S. News and World Report, Fortune*. Occasionally he read *Time* or *Newsweek*. He read the newspaper and the *Dispatcher* primarily for the obituaries. He scattered ashtrays throughout the room.

He started with a clean desk. Reports, brochures, letters, and trivia; he had a vision of papers as high as a mountain. Because Monte had been the secretary-treasurer and then a business agent three times, he had a system for survival. Delegate all the items that had to be reproduced each week or reports that had to be completed monthly. He didn't worry about the bulletin. He tried not to exhaust himself on trivia. He wouldn't worry about who cleaned the office or swept out the parking lot or the million details that swamped each union official.

Monte had field vision, the ability to abstract from all the details and chores, to pinpoint his energies and do only what he must do to stay on top. But always with the personal touch. His votes did not come from memos or piles of paper. They came from long-shoremen. He was good at the face to face, the one on one. Although their problems were exhausting, they were also humorous and exciting. As their legal problems became more complicated, he thought of his relationship to the longshoremen as a play or a charade, a big puzzle and only he had the key part, the one part that kept the ball of wax together. After a troublesome executive board meeting or some ass-kicking meeting at the International, he went off by himself to eat junk food in some out-of-the-way restaurant. This was the way it had been as a business agent. This was the way it had been as the secretary-treasurer three years ago. He didn't expect his method of operating or his way of handling problems to be any different as president.

Monte saturated a rag with furniture polish. He gloried in the slick, mirror finish of the desk. He sat back smoking, then leaned forward to see his image in the brilliance of the desktop.

The phone rang. Dolores, one of the girls in the office, was on the line. "We have a young lady here. She wants to see you. She says she's your niece."

Niece. What a neat touch. Who could she be? Not Katherine. The girls outside knew her. The topless and bottomless dancer that Tijera had lined up for him? She wasn't smart enough to disguise herself as a niece. "Send her in," Monte said. "Wait, is she a blonde?"

"No," Dolores said. "Her hair is pitch black."

"Yeah, yeah, send her in."

When he opened the door, the young girl was already there, tall with a creamy-white face. Not the pale stark white of someone who avoided the sun, but toasty. She wore a loose, summery dress and low white heels. Monte judged her to be seventeen or eighteen years old. Her dark hair was pulled back into a bun. She carried a small white purse and a pair of white gloves in her left hand. She had large luminous brown eyes that didn't drop down but instead concentrated on him. She was distractingly attentive.

Monte was shaking his head to place her.

"I'm Rosalinda," she said. "Joe Karsten's daughter. I'm your niece, Uncle Monte. I'm searching for my father."

"Where's your mom?" Monte asked, stalling.

"She's in Bakersfield, and she's remarried. She has no interest in my father. I'm here alone. I haven't seen my father for twelve years, and I've come to find him."

Now that Maria Teresa was out of the picture, Monte relaxed. But he was puzzled. Why after twelve years and why now?

"Why now?" Monte asked. "Just curious, why now?"

"That's what mother said. After all these years, why now?" As she talked Monte was struck by the evanescent madonnalike quality of her face, the absolute opposite of Sandy's. "I'm going to get married. My mother approves. I want my father to meet the groom, my husband-to-be. I want my father to approve. My mother said that this is archaic. Archaic or not, I want my father to approve."

"If your father doesn't want to see you? He has just remarried. For whatever reason, if he does not want to establish a contact with you?"

"That would end it. I'd go back and marry."

"Why don't we see what we can do." Monte walked around the desk. "Maybe you better give your old Uncle Monte a kiss first. Invite me to the wedding, and I'll come and bring a smashing present to boot." She kissed him on the lips, then placed her cool cheek against his.

He knew Joe had gone back into the Duke of Cream Sherry's gang. Monte called Shedly. The Duke's gang was at Pier Twenty-seven, a short distance from the hall.

"He's close by," Monte said. He walked around and looked closer. "There is a resemblance to your mother, but you're much taller. How is Maria?"

"She's slowed down in recent years. She's an old homebody. This definitely wasn't her idea. My mother's husband is Basque. He owns a small hotel outside of Bakersfield. Mother cooks and helps in the restaurant. Maybe it's the good food or the fresh orange juice that made me so much taller than mother."

"You always were a stringbean," Monte said.

He took Rosalinda through the office and introduced her as his niece to Dolores and Wendy. They drove to Pier Twenty-seven. Monte fully intended to drive onto the pier, but he wasn't sure of Joe's reaction. He parked the car outside and told her to wait by the security shack. He said he'd get Joe and leave the two of them together.

XI *Memories, Dreams, and Nightmares*

When I walked into the sunlight from the shadows of the pier, I saw her. My daughter, my girl. No mistake. She had her mother's hair. The dark hair back in a bun, so Latino. The unmistakable resemblance to Maria Teresa in her face. The way she sat on the wooden bench, so erect, so upright, taller than her mother to be sure. I fought to hold back memories, to hold back the tears. Arms around each other, listening to the sobs, the strokes of her hands across my back. I knew then there would be no recrimination . . . my feelings at first blunted, then expansive, then overwhelming.

I pulled away, holding her at arm's length. The tears rolled down her cheeks, a beautiful girl with a creamy complexion and big brown eyes. The Portuguese influence in the slight curve to her nose, the gypsy look. The trembling chin and the broad forehead. The strength in her arms and the tallness—we almost stood eye to eye. We kissed, smothering each other's lips. Her sobs as she held me tight, her head resting on my shoulder. Then with my fingers embedded in her hair, playfully tossing her head from side to side.

"Lord, oh man, am I glad to see you. My Rosalinda, my little girl."

"Father, I'm not little any more." She ran her arm through mine. With my hands holding her arm as if it were a football and half turned around so we were looking at each other, I hurried her toward my car.

"Are you hungry? Do you want to eat a fish dinner? Do you want to eat at the Eagle Cafe?"

"My stomach is churning inside. I wouldn't be able to eat. You're much better looking than mom described. And trim. I expected a fat little old father, but I didn't care. As long as we are together. We won't lose touch ever again. Never again."

"This is beyond my dreams. Another workday no different from others. What a surprise. My rootbeer-drinking daughter." I pushed her away from me to see her smile, canted and a little crooked. "That beautiful, painful smile."

She confided in me. Her trip to San Francisco was specifically to find me. She was staying at her mother's sister's house at Geneva and Mission. Did I remember Estelle, her mother's sister? Rosalinda was getting married, and I had to approve of the groom. I told her that her taste was good enough for me. I told her about Sandy, that I, too, was married. No problem, I was to come to her wedding and bring my new and lovely wife. Maybe Monte had told her that Sandy was just a few years older than she was.

"I want to meet your wife," Rosalinda said.

"Tonight when she comes home from work," I said. "She'll be surprised."

"I hope she won't be angry."

"Why should she be angry?"

"Paul didn't want me to come up. He thought I was courting disaster. Maybe he was worried that I might divide my affections between my real father and him. Sandy might feel the same."

"I doubt it. When are you getting married?"

"Not for a month . . . it depended on whether I found you or not."

"And your mother's husband. Is he worried about me coming down?"

"Not the slightest. He worries about making money," Rosalinda said. "He's an old man who keeps the restaurant going and makes wine in the basement. He has little interest in me and at times not too much interest in mother. She married him for security."

"I married Sandy for love," I said.

"I'm not hinting that you are insecure, but mother said the longshore industry goes up and down. I want you to approve of the marriage. Does that sound unreasonable to you?"

I hadn't started the car yet. I held her hand. "We are together again. That's all that is important. I'll like Paul. I'll treat your mom fine, even drink her husband's wine. I know you and Sandy will hit it off."

I detected a tightening of her lips, the darkness from her eyes,

now reddened by tears. She wiped her eyes and touched the hand-
kerchief to her nose.

"I hope she likes me," she said.

"Did Monte say anything about her?"

"Only that she was young and attractive and a blonde. That you
two loved each other like a couple of kids."

"Should I call her now? She works at a brokerage house."

"Not yet, father. Wait until later. Can we go to Land's End and
walk the trail back to the Legion of Honor? Remember? That's
our hiding place. Remember how grandmother took a picture of
me against the statue of the lion? First in my dress and then down
to my slip. It was chilly, then freezing cold, and grandmother was a
nut about pictures. She bought me the slip and the dress and
always let me know it. You intervened and said that's enough. My
arms and legs had goose pimples on them. Do you remember,
father? Can we go there?"

"No problem," I said. "We can see the ocean and take our walk.
We'll have supper with Sandy later, and then I'll take you back to
your aunt's place."

Rough waves battered the rocks at Seal Point. Ocean swells
came in, bursting into combers to spray the rocks. All the seals
were in the water, their heads popping up, but the roar of the
combers drowned their barks. Although it was sunny, the promon-
tory was raked by the wind, and it was chilling and cold. I went
into the trunk of my car and took out one of my army jackets—the
ones we bought in the surplus store at the army base—and threw
it around her shoulders without her arms being in the sleeves. A
few tourists used the spectator binoculars, swerving them to take
in the Golden Gate Bridge and the hills in Marin across the channel.
Rosalinda held my hand as we started to hike up the winding
back path toward the Legion of Honor. In some places we had to
step over logs and once even walk the length of a large, slippery
log.

For most of the hike we were silent. The initial burst of tenderness
and love and reaffirmation had died down. We were father and
daughter walking across the broken side of the a hill submerged in
our own thoughts. For me, I recalled the last drunk in·my room
when I thought of her and her mom, the swell of memories that

reemerged whenever I was on a drinking run. How I met Sandy and we had our dance in the sun. My tremendous exhilaration at finding someone to share feelings and love and caresses, to feel I was no longer alone. And now, unbelievable . . . fantastically unbelievable . . . my own daughter had reappeared. My child of those good hiking and fishing and mountain years. We had once camped out in the same place I had taken Sandy, and I had also explained the myriad stars to her. A scene of déjà vu—Maria Teresa asleep inside the station wagon, and my daughter and I on cots under the stars . . . a shooting star and Orion and Cassiopeia and the Big Dipper and the North Star. How the moon was laughing at us because we didn't catch any trout in the Sacramento River that morning. How I stood watch the night the bears came into the campground and beat the garbage cans and overturned them and swished around inside. We woke up at the first streak of dawn, and her mother had a headache so the two of us hiked to the top of Castle Craig. The last two miles were steep, and I told her that vertical walking gave girls strong, shapely legs. How we lost our way and then ran down from the top and sat in the sun on a fallen tree. I explained it had fallen due to lightning or wind or just general erosion. We sat there on the bark of the tree, never imagining that we wouldn't see each other for twelve years.

After the divorce I agreed to stay away, because Maria Teresa complained that it was wrong for a kid to be constantly torn between two parents and victimized by their arguing and fighting. And then, after years went by, I did not want her to see me drinking, never imagining the nightsobs or the desperation Rosalinda felt at the involuntary separation. She only remembered a good father who had cared for her and had feelings for her, a father who was a protector from even her grandma, who had good intentions but always wanted her own way.

I felt Rosalinda's fingers tightening and stroking my fingers. How was I ever so lucky? As Sweetdick said, "We have bad luck, Joe, but luck changes and our turn is coming." My turn came.

The fog closed over us as we neared the Legion of Honor. We walked between the trees. Below us, down the slope, golfers whacked away at golfballs. When she stood in front of the statue of the lion, I noted the trim shape she had acquired from her mother, the low-heeled shoes, the conservative, total nonhippie style about her. The black hair in a bun, held with a barrette.

"I've always had good memories of San Francisco," she said. "Whenever anyone asked where my dad lived . . . I always said, proudly, 'my father lives in San Francisco.' Remember Trudie Steiner pushed me out of a tree and broke both my wrists?"

"Do your wrists hurt?"

"No, never. Wonder where Trudie Steiner went? Wonder if she lives in San Francisco? Father, I'm so glad we discovered each other again. For a long while I thought I'd never see you again . . . not ever. Don't hold anything against mother. She never talked about you much. Whenever I asked, she said, 'He's a hardworking man but not too interested in a home. That's why the marriage broke up.' Then she always added that you had been good to me as a little girl."

I constantly watched the expressions in her face, how her face changed. Maria Teresa was moody, and if Rosalinda was her daughter, she might be half moody. Stereotypes sometimes fit. I had found her, as a child, to be athletic and playful but stubborn, an honest girl with an inordinate amount of curiosity. Press the right button, and she'd fight and scream every time. At times hysteria took over. I had been unable to determine if it was a natural trait or if she had merely picked up on her mother's way of gaining control.

My daughter sat on my jacket on the stone steps under the shadow of the lion, a prim, proper, tastefully dressed young lady. I thought of the old tintypes I had seen of my family—long gone great-grandmothers and great-aunts. Except for the dark hair and flashing eyes, she reminded me of those old tintypes.

She had searched for her father, and whatever I represented was satisfactory to her. The frictions between us would be minimal. She hadn't come to settle a vendetta. Her goal, simple and uncomplicated, to see if blood could rekindle love.

She reminded me of Maria Teresa in her younger days, before Maria Teresa became a basket case. Maybe Rosalinda viewed me as the underdog in the marriage with Maria Teresa and wanted to rewrite the injustice, although I had been insensitive to her mother's demands. I always had the idea that the headaches and the back problems and all her ailments might get better if she would wake up each morning with a determination to quit being moody and to make the day sunny and joyful. But how was I to know Rosalinda's inner thoughts? When fathers are long gone, girls in their romantic stage make heroes of them. Invariably what they discover when they find them is a hero with clay feet.

What had she expected? A short, fat dockworker, some half-smashed drunk who'd make her nostrils creep with his bad breath from stale cigarette smoke and cheap whiskey? Someone who would feed her ears with whiskey lies and recriminations toward her mother with buckets of self-pity and resentments? If she had arrived earlier, she would have seen a fat-fingered, booze-bloated father adrift in a detox center. There were two or three fathers in the same body, and she had been lucky; she had found the right one. As we walked back to the car under the spirals of fog, I couldn't remember if I had ever told Sandy I had a daughter.

Rosalinda was surprised at all the Chinese on Clement Street. "I didn't know the city had two Chinatowns."

"This area is called Chinatown West," I said. "They have been moving in and buying everything in sight for hard American cash."

"I notice you don't have a house," she said, laughing, as if to confirm her mother's description of our reason for separating.

"Sandy and I are in the process of buying a house."

"I'm glad for you . . . I can hardly wait to meet her."

Sandy came home from work, skipping stairs as she came up. When she saw Rosalinda sitting among the packed boxes and the disarray of the flat, she stopped dead.

"Sandy, this is my daughter, Rosalinda. Sweetie, this is my wife."

The chill set in from the start. The formalities were taken care of rapidly. Rosalinda was to be married. She searched for her father, a father she hadn't seen in twelve years. Standard operating procedure—father gives away the bride, then we all go home and live our own lives. But I sensed that Sandy thought of Rosalinda as competition, a goody-goody girl who might pour on the poor-child-who-had-been-discarded routine. Please take me back into your arms, daddy dear. Rosalinda was a threat to the home in Noe

Valley and the rose-and-carnation dance in the sun, a short, lively dance disrupted by a troublesome memory from the past. How do you combat blood?

Sandy smiled and touched Rosalinda's hand, and for a quick moment they held their arms around each other. In my daughter's eyes I saw a different picture. To her Sandy must look like a floaty hippie tramp searching for a home, free meals, and an older man she could twirl around her little finger. How did this healthy young girl hardly older than herself talk this naive man into her hoax, her game, her meal ticket. Rosalinda's Latin coloring, bearing, and trim, Sunday-school way of dressing could be upsetting to Sandy, just as Sandy's loose dresses, swinging skirts, sandals, face tanned by the sun, unpolished nails, and short, uncombed chopped hair could appear odd to my straitlaced daughter. I sensed the antagonism and the chill, but I wasn't bothered by it. Rosalinda would rationalize . . . if father finds this child-woman responsive to him and he loves her, then she must be good. To her there would be no battle of possession. She had never been cloying or jealous, even in her worst childhood hysterics.

We had dinner at a new French place on Geary Boulevard. The meal was adequate, and we finished two bottles of wine with the meal. Rosalinda nursed one drink, and I was glad to see her sip wine.

"I'm troubled by all the French names," Rosalinda said. "We speak Portuguese at home. I'm sure if I learned Chinese and Italian, I'd be able to communicate with all the waiters and cooks in San Francisco. I'm not used to a big, metropolitan city, with all these nationalities."

I noticed a smile appear on Sandy's face that said, why do I need to worry about this Jehovah's Witness, this pamphlet-pushing, small-town hick. To her, Rosalinda was a square. And Rosalinda probably didn't see the Bighorn Mountains or Wyoming when she looked at Sandy. She focused on the disheveled blonde hair and that funky attitude that Sandy always exuded.

After dinner I asked Sandy if she wanted to drive with us while I took Rosalinda to her Aunt Estelle's.

"I'm sure that you want to talk to your daughter alone. I'll do some more packing."

I drove Rosalinda to her aunt's, but I didn't go inside. I suggested that I'd take the next day off and we'd spend the entire day together.

When I came home I saw that Sandy had been drinking. No extra boxes were packed, our clothes strewn all over, and books off the shelves and stacked on the floor. Dishes were out of the cupboard but on the kitchen table. I loaded one box with plates and salad dishes and our collection of mismatched cups. I went into our room. "Hey, why all the drinking?"

"You drink during the day," she said.

"Yes, but only a few beers and never at night without you."

"Have a drink," she said. She poured gin into a glass and threw in a few ice cubes. One cube caromed off the table onto the floor. She splashed in ginger ale so carelessly that most of it spilled from the table to the floor. "Families who drink together stay together, now that you have your little girl. God, what a prude."

"Sandy, button up. I know it's only the liquor talking, but what does she have to do with us? She didn't come here to break us up. She has a life of her own. She's getting married next month. Don't say things you'll be sorry for, something I can't handle."

"I can handle us being alone. I married you, not the rest of your family."

"No one's asking you to be a stepmother."

I thought this was just a tiff. Tomorrow she'd be sorry. If necessary I'd make sure there was a minimum of contact between her and my daughter. But it puzzled me. Was this jealousy or just a spoiled-brat form of getting her way?

"I'm going to take a bath."

That was a good sign. Perhaps we'd have one of our games and relax into the euphoria that comes after sex.

While she was in the shower I drank slowly. I noticed the .38 on the nightstand by the telephone, the oiling kit on the floor. I checked the closet. The long-barreled .22 was still in a cardboard box in the corner. Thoughtfully I checked the cupboard. There were the pills for her back, and others, too, a collection of uppers and downers. On the label . . . Presbyterian Clinic . . . Thelma Jo Bonner. She was still getting the pills in her maiden name. I located the date. These were from before we married. Doctor Sam Cullum. I knew him to be a psychiatrist. We had talked about the pills a couple of times. I didn't like her taking them, but she always had an answer, a reason for every pill.

I heard her singing in the bathroom. Soon we'll be in our own home. All her insecurities and mine will vanish, I decided. We'll live happily ever after, I said to no one in particular, as I poured another shot of gin into the empty glass.

When she came out of the bathroom, she took two pills with a glass of water and headed for bed. She didn't say, Come to bed. I didn't ask her if she wanted me to. Leave well enough alone. A night's sleep might clear the air.

I had two more drinks before I turned in. I went to bed in her former room but stayed awake for only a short time. It had been a long, exciting day, plus the drinking made me tired. I knew I forgot to set the alarm, and was not even sure if Sandy had.

In the morning I heard her stirring in the kitchen, but by the time I came out she was gone. I searched for the checkbook. She had taken it with her. I called the hall for a replacement, and the dispatcher gave me static for calling so late. I really didn't care whether he replaced me or not. The Duke of Cream Sherry would cover me, send a holdman up to hook on with Borrego. If they were under pressure, the Duke would go onto the dock and hook on himself. He had done it many times.

I parked on the hill by the Cliff House. Rosalinda and I went down to the esplanade that ran the entire length of the ocean front. We walked onto the beach and stayed just out of reach of the eddies of water.

"I detected a certain coolness from Sandy," Rosalinda said. "I hope that I didn't disrupt your marriage. I want to be her friend. Father, you and I are going to see each other again. We're not going to allow all the water to go under the bridge for another twelve years, are we?"

"Sandy must be peeved because I lied to her," I said. "When she asked me if I had any children, I said no. I'll never know why I told her that. Maybe because we were in a detox, and she meant nothing to me at that time. I thought I'd never see her again, and it really wasn't any of her business. Now don't you be angry at me for that lie."

"I didn't come four hundred miles to be angry at you."

"Even if Sandy remains cool to you, it won't stop me from seeing you. You're my daughter, not some flaky girl on a rescue mission. She has to accept that. I'm coming to the wedding, alone if necessary. Bet your bottom dollar on that."

"What's that man doing over there?" Rosalinda asked. "The man walking ahead of us. He's touching all the metal cans."

"That's the metal man. He walks along the waterfront, too, and touches the rails and the wheels of the freight cars. Fire hydrants, the tops of the cars. He even caresses the steel beams that hold up the freeway."

"Is he crazy?"

"No, not dangerous crazy. He just has this one kick." I watched him go up the stone steps and sweep his hand along the protective railing. "One of my friends, Borrego Red, told me he was a marine fireman involved in a boiler explosion aboard ship, and he's checking to see if the metal is hot. Someone else said that he was a longshoreman involved in some kind of accident that had to do with steel beams. Nothing checks out. He's as much a mystery now as he was years ago."

He disappeared from sight.

"What's he doing now?" Rosalinda asked.

"Maybe running his hands over the tops of cars parked up there."

"There are a lot of weird people in this city," Rosalinda said.

We walked past a few surf fishermen. Two riders came by on horses. Another man had a big Labrador retriever, and when he threw a stick, the dog splashed into the surf to find it, bouncing back onto the beach each time.

"Hopefully you and your wife both can come down to the wedding," Rosalinda continued. "She's so young. It's hard for me to call her your wife. I guess she's what they call a hippie?"

"Don't you have any hippies in Bakersfield?"

"No," she said tonelessly. "We're a million miles behind times."

"Her name's Thelma Jo," I said. "Yes, Jo, same as mine but without the *e*. She favors the name Sandy. She was born in Wyoming, in a small town near the Bighorn Mountains. She's country. She can cook, sew her own clothes. She's had a hard life. Don't judge her too harshly."

"I don't want to judge her at all," Rosalinda said. "I want to be friends. We are not competitors. I'm not going to be piling in on you forever, trying to disrupt your life."

"Don't think that," I said. "Our coming together is so natural. I've been dreamy about my own father for years. He was lost in a mine disaster. If you knew how many times I started to come to see you. How I procrastinated and procrastinated. I still have only one photo of you. The others have disappeared. God, everything seems to peel away and disappear. But I never lost the one of you sitting on the stone statue, pouting and freezing cold."

"I have oodles of photographs, and I didn't bring any. Not a blasted one. The idea to see you was always in my head, but coming up was on the spur of the moment."

"Sandy is a little upset, but she'll get over it. She's not stupid. Given time, she'll come around. We can all be friends without piling on top of each other in some kind of fantasy hayrack."

"I'm going home in two days," she said. "Is that okay with you? When I leave, can you drive me to the bus station? I'll ride at night so I can sleep all the way."

"No sweat. I may work tomorrow. If I do, I'll see you tomorrow night. We can go over to see Monte and your Aunt Pamela. I'll try to smooth things over with Sandy, but I'm not going to make a United Nations project out of it. She has to understand that I've neglected you enough. That we want to simply be what we are— related by blood. She's my wife, and you're my daughter. If she still wants some time to stay in the closet and pout, she can have it. We'll visit Monte's place by ourselves."

"Don't press her, father. She's had a shock. Give her time to absorb it. I'm sure everything will be okay."

We came to the esplanade near the zoo and had cheeseburgers and chili in a small café. I got carried away and even bought a cigar.

"I took a risk," Rosalinda said. "I play hunches, and my hunch said that you and I would get along. I remembered that you never hit me and even mother said you didn't. She said you'd never use a babysitter. One time while I was still a baby, mother said you took me over to Uncle Monte's to play poker. You had me on a pillow in a drawer behind you within reach of your chair, and Uncle Monte asked, 'Doesn't all the cigarette and cigar smoke and fumes from the alcohol hurt her?' And you answered, 'Maybe.

But if there's a fire back at the house and I lost her, I'd never forgive myself.' Monte asked, 'What if there's a fire here?' Mother said you answered, 'If we didn't get out of the house, everyone we loved was in one room, and we'd all go together.'" Rosalinda leaned across the table and kissed me smack on the mouth. "That incident out of our past had as much to do with coming to see you as any other."

We walked on the sidewalk going back. The distance seemed much longer. The wind had come up, and it was chilly. I drove her home and agreed to call her the next day.

I went directly home after dropping off my daughter. I entertained the idea of going into Hakk's or O'Shea's for a drink, but there was already enough hassle with Sandy. All I found in the flat was a bottle of vodka three-quarters full. I disliked vodka, but Sandy liked it because it had no taste. After a few drinks, I called the brokerage house. I had expected to surprise her, as she worked on the switchboard. Another girl answered and said that Sandy had not been in that day. She offered no explanation. I decided that when Sandy came in, I'd pretend she had come from work. I had taken off work many times. I was not going to make an issue out of it.

At eight o'clock, many ideas crossed my mind. Should I call the police? Something I'd never done. Call the city's emergency line? No. I was tired of vodka and went out to buy a bottle of Fleischmann's gin. As a second thought I bought a bottle of barbera wine, too. There was some stew in the refrigerator, enough for the two of us. I thought of making a large salad, but I didn't. Johnny had gone to visit his mother in Chinatown and wouldn't come in at all or if he did, it would be late. I sat, drinking and waiting.

She came in at nine. I heard her fumbling at the door and her feet scraping each step as she came up the long flight of stairs.

"Where have you been?" I tried to keep anger out of my voice.

"Been nowhere." She was really unstable. "Nowhere, nowhere." Her eyes were funny, and she didn't sit down but toddled across the room to the cupboard and all the pills. I poured another drink for myself. I was puzzled over her reaction to something as natural and necessary as the visit from my daughter. Our short dance had really been short.

"Sit down," I said. I walked over and took the pill container from her but not fast enough to keep her from swallowing two pills. I never had the temperament to be around pillheads, hadn't even thought to ask her if she still used pills while we were in the detox center. She was a user, all right. They had come into the house slowly but steadily. Two bottles one day, another the next, until we had a menagerie of pills. And now I had a drunken and up-high woman on my hands. "No more of this bullshit," I warned. "Sit down. I want to talk to you. Where have you been?"

"I don't want to talk."

"Where have you been?"

"Where have you been?" She imitated me.

"Don't give me that pillhead crap. I'm asking you. Where've you been?"

"Working, where else? One of the girls had a birthday party, and we went out for a few drinks."

"A few drinks. . . . You're so stupid silly that you can hardly stand up. Besides, I called the office."

"I'm my own woman, and I went to visit a few old friends. You have plenty of friends, and I have plenty of friends, and never the twain shall meet." She giggled and slobbered.

"Why don't we go to bed. We can talk tomorrow. I don't want to get mad."

"Get as mad as you want. I'm leaving. For good. That girl last night was just too much."

"What girl?"

"Your daughter. Telling me a sad story, how your wife left you . . . never mentioning a daughter. She appears out of nowhere . . . twirls you around her thumb."

"She isn't twirling me around her thumb. She wanted to be friends with you. She sensed your coldness. What in the conceivable hell do you have against her? She's nothing to you."

"That's right. She's nothing to me. You can have your little sweety-pie and her old-fashioned dresses and the fake-religious way she has of talking. She must buy her clothes in a secondhand thrift shop."

"She's not fake religious. She's a Catholic. Besides, she didn't even mention religion. Religion has nothing to do with it. You may be more religious than she is."

"I'm leaving anyway. I'm fed up, and it won't work anyhow. I took a good look at you last night and a better look now. A tired old man. I'm on my way. I'm not riding this horse anymore."

"Leave if you must." I was tired of talking. I knew the futility of talking to someone out of her mind on some kind of pills and heavily sedated with booze. One drug just fed the other.

"I'm leaving and not where you think I'm going. You won't be able to follow me. You can have your little Miss Muffet, though I doubt she's ever even seen a spider."

"Don't act so subnormal."

She went into the other room and was stuffing something in her purse. Her dress was dark, and she had on a blue sweater. I heard the rain splatter on the roof. Typical San Francisco weather. Sun and fog and then rain. Three seasons in one day. I envisioned her crossing the streets in the rain and dark, a target for cars at every crosswalk. "What are you doing?"

"I'm going outside."

"No, not in this rain, not in the condition you're in." She shambled toward the door, and I grabbed her.

"Keep your filthy hands off me."

"Not until you're in your right mind. Stay home and go to sleep. Tomorrow, when the pills and booze wear off, you can leave. I promise. I won't stop you."

"There is no tomorrow. I'm going now."

She tried to struggle from my grasp. I carried her into the bedroom, slammed her down on the bed. "No bullshit. You can't leave tonight, not in those dark clothes in the rain. No one will see you stumbling across the street. I won't have your maimed body or your death on my conscience."

"That's your worry. Your beloved conscience and a broken-down old dream that drifts in from the valley. What happened to us? Remember, we live for each other, and we'll always be together? Just the two of us, buddies and companions? I believed all that crap. If you could only see yourself now . . . lying on me. That's what you are, an old man lying on a young girl, and I still have young-girl ideas."

I had no counter for that. My mind had become clear. How had it all started? What if I allowed her to go out? What if she did leave for good? The evenings at home, the perfume, her bare body under the raincoat as we walked arm in arm. Bubbles in an empty frame. How would I handle the lonesome evenings, more lonesome now that I had a taste of the sun? What crazy actions. Did I expect to keep her locked up as a reluctant mummy and hope for the best, hope that tomorrow we'd be straight and clear headed? We might be able to talk things out. Even with all this irrationality on her part, we could still compromise. She need not see Rosalinda again. It was no big thing for her to miss the wedding. She made feeble attempts to struggle and squirm out of my grasp, but I held her tight.

"Quit trying to struggle, and I'll let you get up. Promise me you won't go out until you have a few cups of coffee?"

"I'm not promising anything. Get your stupid overweight body off me. I'll do anything I want to do."

Then she bit me, catching two fingers as I held her mouth. I had wanted to keep her from screaming. My fingers were bleeding, and as I retracted my hand she began to struggle harder. I thought about tying her up, but there was no rope and string wouldn't hold her. Maybe if I grabbed one of her stockings and got it around her hands or just smeared her once, a left hook or a bolo punch. One wallop to the chin to knock her out. It wasn't in me to do it. Even locking her in the room was no solution—there were windows. And if she started screaming, we'd be in a worse mess.

"Hold still," I said.

I was trying to get in a better position, hold her down and stop the blood from my fingers from staining the bedspread. I had put myself off balance. She heaved, and I fell to the floor while she sprang from the bed, tearing into her purse. She had the gun . . . the short-nosed .38. I was half seated and half sprawled in the way of the door. I was conscious that she might charge out the door, and I had covered that exit. But exits were not important anymore.

"Why the gun?" I asked. "If you want to shoot, go ahead and shoot."

"Joe . . . " she began to sob. "The gun's not for you. Oh, Joseph. . . . Please believe me, the gun's not for you."

"To kill Rosalinda?" I asked.

"Even now you refuse to understand . . . so foolishly refuse to understand. I had no intention of harming you or harming her. Why didn't you just let me go? Just let me walk out."

"With a gun . . . you hardly know how to shoot, and why the gun anyway? Talk to me, Sandy. What have I done to you? How are we in this mess? Give me the gun, and we'll talk about it in the morning." Keep talking but get the gun.

"There will never be a morning."

I was totally baffled. What did she mean, the gun was not for me? Then who was it for? Did she intend to stick up a bank or did she have some old pimp boyfriend waiting in the wings? I discounted the bank and the pimp, but nothing was sure. The events of the last two days made me more unsure than ever before.

I tried to remain clear in my head. I wasn't afraid of her. She wasn't that good a shot, and with both of us scrambling, it would be an even race. But I didn't want the gun to go off accidentally. Now I questioned her sanity . . . not her total sanity but her immediate sanity. I had to keep calm. Joke her out of it, but get the gun. It all seemed so incongruous.

"Sandy, please sit down. Topple over accidentally and that goddamed gun will go off and the neighbors will think . . ."

Tears streaming down her face and coughing. "Who the hell cares about the neighbors? You care. Maybe that politico brother of yours cares. Maybe that small-town ancient-dressed little girl of yours cares. I care hell about neighbors. I want to go. Please let me go."

"Not with the gun. Throw it over. Better still, lay it down on the bed, and I'll let you walk through this door. We can see each other in the morning. Lay it down."

Whenever I made a move to stand up, she tightened her finger on the trigger, and her face became distorted. Not with hatred. I didn't pick up any hatred.

There was always a worry with people who hadn't been around guns much. One shot, and they were sorry. But after that shot, all sorrys were too late.

I tried to sit up.

"Don't try to jump me, Joe. Don't do something you'll be sorry for. Dearest, I don't want to hurt you. Crawl over to the window, away from the door, and give me a minute. I'll leave the gun on the bottom stair. I promise. Please do that, and there'll be no problem. Just let me leave the house, and I'll do just as I promised. The gun

will be on the bottom stair. I'm beginning to change my mind
. . . I'm on a different track. I'm not worried about the gun. Just
let me get away. I can't explain what is happening. Tomorrow you
can meet me. Tonight I want to be by myself and away from you.
Away from all the shopping and cooking and being so good and so
clean . . . your daughter is everything I hate and love at the same
time. I want to go my way for a little while until my head gets
clear from all the hatred that I don't understand. I beg of you,
please let me go. I don't want to hurt you in any way, and I won't
hurt you. The gun was not meant for you."

Keep her talking . . . "If the gun isn't meant for me, who is it
for? For some old boyfriend?" I said this coaxingly, not believing it
myself. "For someone I don't know? Some old score to settle? You
don't have to tell me. Just lay down the gun, and we can talk it out
and settle it. But I can't do anything lying here on the rug. I'm
beginning to feel foolish, and what if Johnny comes home?"

"Johnny told us yesterday he would be visiting his mother and
staying at her place overnight. Johnny's not a problem. If I can
walk out, I'll give you the gun. But not in here. I'll leave it at the
bottom of the stairs, and then I'll be gone. Don't wait for me. Joe,
I'm never coming back."

"Don't be foolish. We're going to straighten this out. I love you,
and my daughter's visit has nothing to do with us staying together.
I'll be understanding, not judgmental. It's hardly fair for me to be
down on the floor and have you standing there with Borrego's gun.
If I get up and it goes off accidentally? So it wasn't meant for me.
But I'll be a dead son of a bitch, and you'll be jumping on my
coffin as they lower it into the grave, jumping on my coffin in
ballet leotards with a bunch of red roses and people will say she
loved him so much she wanted to go to the grave with him and so
young, too."

"Stop, please stop. . . . I'm going to throw the gun out the
window."

"No, wait. Don't do that."

If I could only distract her for a minute. I was on one knee,
watching the trigger. I no longer cared if she blew a hole in the
floor. I was tired of arguing. I no longer wanted to play some long,
stupid waiting game. I'd stake everything on one charge and grab

for the gun. If it shot up the ceiling, okay. Even if it shot into the floor, as long as it didn't kill my Chinese landlord or one of his very surprised customers.

She stood there, tears drying on her face and eyes bright, cold, and hazy all at the same time.

I leaped and we struggled over the gun, as I tried to wrench it from her grasp, twist it loose from her fingers. I almost had it. Then, the explosion. I reacted with a jerk, but it had not hit me. She sank from my arms to the floor. The deep, darkening wet of her dress above the stomach. The enlarging stain of blood blending in with the blue of the dress. I laid her down gently, my hands taking the gun from her fingers that were now as limp as her body, aware that my prints had covered all of her prints on the gun. She was pale with a raspy cough, as I placed a pillow under her head.

"The gun wasn't for you." Her voice feeble and low. "Nor for your daughter. It's a joke for you to bring up some old flame. I meant the gun for me, Joe, to get me out of the way. I'm no good for you . . . Joe, Joe."

Call a doctor. Call Kaiser. What was the emergency number? I listened for someone running up the stairs. All I heard was the traffic from the street. The squeak of brakes, the cars gunning ahead. I was going to release her head from the cradle of my arm and call the hospital. Her neck gave a crick, and she went totally limp. I felt the wrist. No pulse. Listened for her breathing. She was dead. I felt for her heart again as she lay there, pale face drooped as a rag doll. The blood a puddle at her side. I have been around dead people many times, I said to no one in particular. Sandy was dead. And I sat there holding her poor raggedy-doll body, and I froze, immobilized, not knowing what to do. No one would ever believe me. Not even Rosalinda. She had guessed something was wrong but had no understanding of what.

I waited as if time might alter the circumstances, and she'd start breathing again. There was no doubt. She had that peculiar limpness that comes before the body stiffens. I knew it was useless, but I felt her heart again and then put my ear to her chest. Nothing. No pulse. Nothing, only a dead girl. Sandy gone.

I knew I had to call someone. Monte. Misplaced understanding. Rosalinda. My daughter had had enough shocks in two days. I knew I had to call someone, but the longer I waited the harder it was to reach the door and go into the other room to the phone. I wanted to take the gun away from her body, but I didn't want to touch it. My prints were all over the gun. If I wiped them clean the police would know someone had wiped them clean. Who? Certainly not the poor dead girl, stretched out on the floor.

I went into the other room. Instead of going to the phone, I poured a stiff drink of gin, the liquid splashing my trembling hands. My cold body shaking, so cold I found myself with a blanket over my shoulders sitting in the chair, trying to get the gin inside me to calm me down. I no longer thought about the phone. Phone who? Dead is dead. A phone call wouldn't solve anything. I laid my head against the top of the heavily cushioned armchair. Startled from my trance to drink gin and, between drinks, sobbing.

XII *The Strike*

Monday morning. His mahoganied office. The union standard and the American flag on a stand in the corner. Pictures of the union hierarchy on the walls. The telephone banging off the table. Monte answered. "Did what? They all walked off. Hold on . . . can you get them back?" He heard Tijera's voice screaming at the other end.

"Most of them have gone home and the hardheads are in front of the piers and giving the teamsters and anyone going through a hard time." Tijera talking. "Monte, you got to come down."

Jesus Christ. The caucus and convention only a month away and the longshoremen jumped the gun and shut down the port. Everyone knew the port was rampant with dissatisfaction, but no one believed these new kids had the guts to do it. Harry Bridges screaming. No one was satisfied with the impending contract or with loading diverted cargo from the East Coast. Rumors sliced across the docks, but there were always rumors. Monte had judged there would be a lot of voice but no action. He was wrong. President of the local and under personal pressure to play the game, at least if he had any intention of reaching for the top. The Coast Committee the next rung on the ladder, and now the longshoremen and gearmen and even some of the steady men jumped the gun and shut down the port. The main issue was over the steady men. The issue had split the union in two. Plus, most members wanted the two coasts—the ILWU and the ILA—to have contracts that expired at the same time. The East Coast was on strike at this time, and Monte agreed that working the diverted cargo was a sophisticated way of scabbing.

Monte grabbed his hat. He had to get out there and find out who the shit disturbers were. But he had already had a transformation. If you can't beat them, join them. He had misjudged the wave of support for the shutdown of the port. Bring things to a head. Not wait for the International and the bureaucrats to water down the demands and make agreements that were legal and binding and tied the longshoremen's hands with arbitrations and grievance procedures. The longshoremen had decided Monte's direction of action. He had to take off and take command. It was a risk, but faint heart never won fair lady. Monte rushed out the door.

XIII *Journey to the End of the Bottle*

And here I was back at the same old stand. Selling the same old
blues. The bar at the lower end of Clement Street was one I didn't
ordinarily inhabit. I sat on the stool a zombie hooked and wired to
the dead body in my room drinking drink after drink barely
conscious of the pool table and the pool balls clicking and the
interplayer squabbling. Not conscious of the cockroaches that
crossed the bar, the beery and antiseptic smell of the bar. I had
seen the bartender around Clement Street, jockey sized and a
drinker, now working in an alcoholic fog dispensing drinks but
unable to function as a judge or jury for the squabbles over the
pool game. He stood behind the bar, his head barely above it,
moving as if he was on roller skates. Packs of Winstons were
evenly spaced behind the bar, so he was never more than a hand's
reach from a smoke. Exhaling smoke from his nostrils, George-
Raft style. No women were in the bar. The man next to me had
started a conversation with me two or three times, bewildered by
my inability to respond. He was talking again. Although the
lighting was low key, I had a clear picture of him.

"I'm not an intelligent person." His pants were up, his shoes
had no laces, and he had no socks on at all. Probably unwashed
feet, but there was no way to tell in the shaded light. Coming
closer, his head toward mine. "I hold the rank of colonel in
intelligence."

He mumbled between drinks. Obviously he was interested in
what I did. What if I told him that I was in some measure responsible for the death of a young girl? That she lay stone cold dead on
a broken-down Persian carpet in a bedroom above a liquor store.
He would absorb it with the drunken finesse only barroom addicts
have. It might even be interesting. If I asked him what to do with
the body, he'd probably have advice. Maybe a brother-in-law, a
captain in the same intelligence network who disposed of dead
bodies. An authority who disposed of dead bodies without the

authorities knowing. I knew he'd soon ask me what I did, and to remove him from my concentration, I told him. "I'm a commodore in the navy, and I'm on a secret mission. I have no time for games." That ended our brief talk. He needed someone to play out the fantasy string with him. I didn't need to talk and my attitude said so.

The bars changed, but the need to be alone did not. I wanted to keep my mind off Sandy and what I was to do about her body. How fast would she deteriorate? The smell alone might bring Johnny in. Just move all my books and clothes and pretend she was not there? Talk to someone about it? Ask for advice? The colonel in intelligence? The director of the Hetch-Hetchy Reservoir? The ranger in charge of Lava Beds National Monument?

Infantry privates never drink in bars. I've never met a man in a bar who wasn't at least a captain, and the rank always elevated with each drink. Not many hod carriers, either, but buckets of superintendents who usually sit at the end of the bar away from the cash register. For some I might be a murderer, when in fact I knew I was not. And every drink relieved the problem . . . if there really was a problem . . . something easily solved in the morning . . . if there ever will be a morning.

I drank at two bars on Balboa, then transferred to Geary Boulevard and worked my way down to the bar across from Sears. I glanced at the Band-Aids on my two fingers, where Sandy had bit me. When had I put them on? The idea of getting a tetanus shot suddenly interrupted . . . coming to my senses. Why worry about pissant bites on my fingers and tetanus shots when I had a dead body in my room?

I had been drinking gin and vodka most of the night, and now I ordered a Manhattan. Some drinkers like Monte, who are not serious drinkers at all, always order the same drink—VO straight or over the rocks. Zack was forever stuck on Early Times. Most drinkers have one preference. My drinks changed with my moods and with the drained-out tiredness of drinking the same drink. I had scary and complete recall of certain incidents in my life but was never able to recall my previous drinks. Was it vodka and seven or grapefruit or gin and orange? I loved brandy in the morning, spike the coffee, an old Italian standby—coffee royal. I was interested in bourbon. That is the correct phrasing . . . I was interested in bourbon and more than interested in Scotch and not as interested in blended whiskey. Bourbon de Luxe and Kessler. He who hasn't vomited to Kessler hasn't vomited at all. Down the line. Tokay . . . all the way with Santa Fe tokay. Petri took time to make a good wine. Grey Shadow white port, how elegant can you get? Muscatel, can't stand it. Why can't I stand it? I can't answer that question, but I know I can't. I've never gotten low enough to appreciate muscatel. Barbera, yes. Cabernet Sauvignon, yes, how elegant. Chardonnay gold, what a gas. Start high is my motto. Never go underpowered.

Walking. I knew where I wanted to go. Down to the bars near the wharf, not the bars across from the docks, as most of them closed late at night. My clothes were clean, and I was clean shaven and had some money. The checkbook from her purse and my bankbook in the back pocket of my pants. But I had to get down where there was immediate money. Drinking exhausted money fast.

If I thought of Sandy, a lump came into my throat and I felt the beginning of tears. I was nowhere near the tear-faced boozy stage that would come later. One didn't cry in the bars in the avenues. A few cried in the bars along Howard and Mission. There were no tears in the bars of the Tenderloin—too sleazy, too furtive, too hip with everyone on the make. I imagined the fag bars on Polk Street awash with tears, but I didn't know for sure.

I took a cab to the Miramar Cafe, where an old walking-boss friend of Monte's hung out. They called him Tango because he was punchy and quick on his feet. He had an offbeat style. He knew how to bullshit across the board—talk pidgin Spanish to the Latinos from the Mission and motherfucker talk to the Blacks from the Fillmore, infuse pride in the Portuguese from the Flats on the west side of Oakland, bullshit about lying down in front of a troop train for the hippie longshoremen and then tell them he'd buy them whiskey and yogurt at the Black Cat after work. I'm talking about longshoremen, now. I didn't know what kind of bullshit he used on uptown and downtown people. He was allegedly a high-class drinker, if drinking in a mod tourist fern bar across from the Dolphin Club might be considered high class.

I didn't want to call Monte, and I knew Tango carried a big roll. A California bankroll, a fifty-dollar bill wrapped around a lemon.

He was a friend of Monte's and consequently a secondhand friend of mine. His one peculiarity—he didn't drink around longshoremen. Hence the hangout in the Miramar. Sip an Irish coffee and watch the cable cars turn around. On the job he had the longshoremen buffaloed. He was the boss, and they had to listen to his bullshit. In a bar and drunk out of their minds and unable to cop to his bullshit, they might deck him, just start swinging. He had a rep as a club fighter from years ago, but no one had put him to the test in years, not since the time he had turned over the People's World float in a Labor Day parade and the reds worked him over.

I found him in the Miramar Cafe holding court with two tourist ladies. He didn't want to give me money in front of them, so we arranged to meet in the can. He took his time coming, so I read the graffiti . . . *Howard Goldstein is a Neo Classicist . . . Laverne thinks of her body as a temple . . . Que Toda La Vida Es Sueno, Y Los Suenos Suenos Son—Calderon de La Barca* . . . I didn't understand the Spanish and I didn't know the man's name . . . *Take a homosexual to lunch.* Most of it wasn't readable, except for big scratches on the walls and a few telephone numbers over the urinal, hinting that a person who dialed the numbers could get his cock sucked. There was no hint about whether the numbers belonged to men or women.

When Tango came down the steps, he told me he'd appreciate my not butting in with his women. I told him I needed money, not women, that I had bad luck with women. That's an understatement. Tango loaned me two twenties, enough for the rest of the night. He told me that's all he could give me because the piers were shut down—I didn't know what he was talking about. I'd go to the bank in the morning and then call Monte or Rosalinda and try to explain Sandy's death. I pushed her from my mind. Whenever I thought of her, I became sick.

I had a drink in the Miramar, cashing one of the twenties from Tango and sitting four stools from him watching his action. Tango holding his seance, the two ladies hooked on his bullshit or maybe, if they were observant, hooked on the leather boots and the cashmere sport jacket and the Spanish leather wallet crammed full of bills. There was nothing wrong in Tango handling his life in this manner, but he had a wife and six kids in Bernal Heights and a grammar-school education plus a few punchy tours of gyms and lowlife auditoriums. So, Tango, I owe you forty dollars that you'll never get back. I had an inkling of that, even at the time. He was another yacht club commodore or colonel in intelligence. The only difference was that Tango had a high-paying job.

This little oasis wasn't my oasis, but I didn't know where to go. I ordered another Yellowstone on the rocks. Perhaps I'd make this my steady drink, like Tango with his Irish coffee or Monte with the VO. I remembered Sandy loved red wine, and every so often a sweet cognac. Where had she acquired that taste? Perhaps in the Brown Derby or the Coconut Grove, the only two places I knew in Hollywood. Not my hangouts, especially at the Beverly Hills end of Sunset Boulevard near the music studios, where the girls ply their wares. What an artificial way of saying they are whores and fuck for dough. They are all young and fashionable; a few are young and hippie. They stir the blood of older movie executives driving by in their big cars. The financial and emotional bargaining at the curb. The girls in raincoats, fashionable raincoats worn as an insignia or uniform. It never fucking rains in Hollywood. They make their contracts right along the curb . . . fifty scoots for a half and half, seventy-five for a tongue bath, maybe a hundred for spankings and all the crazy velvety crap they think up. I assume the hookers paddled the executives' asses. The girls are too smart to have their asses sizzled by some sadist, unless their beauty has faded and they take the leftovers.

Some were knockouts. Sandy would attest to that. Although she came from Wyoming and had the mood and temperament of a rodeo girl, she had the face of a steamy tart. When she was sixteen or seventeen, she turned on those fake producers. Everyone is fake, so why shouldn't Hollywood be fake. If we have stupid commodores in stupid bars in the avenues and colonels of intelligence walking Skid Row and walking bosses wearing cashmere sport coats and Gucci cuff links, hoodwinking the tourists with only a grammar-school education, then what must it be like on Sunset Boulevard? Movie stars and studio producers sweet-talking the young girls from the farms, the rodeo and hippie swingers who had never lucked out in Wyoming but spent their childhoods dodging uncles and stepfathers and sleazy old men who had fuck city on their minds.

To climb on some fake-stepfather's lap and he's playing a role

. . . pretending . . . "patty cake, patty cake" . . . having a hard-on tickling a small child's backside. Maybe even coming and pushing her off his lap, pretending again that it is late and he has no time for play and has to get to the bathroom to wipe the semen from his pants. Or pretending he has spilled water on himself. The lecher. I know it's old-fashioned to call them lechers in this new computerized Freudian zoo. They have other words for them, but I didn't know the words. This lecher asking the bemused and ever-so-small Sandy if she knows this game, inside and outside the fence candy game. She shuts her eyes, stroking the thumb and cock until she has his wet job. She stands there with her cupped hand full of milky white sperm.

I had to get out of this place. All this bodyshop talk made me goofy in the head.

The cab dropped me off at a bar on the rim of the Tenderloin. Big, bulky transvestites paraded on the street in front of the bar, silly frocks high above their soccer legs. Crowds of kids in Levis. Young girls wearing painters' overalls. Both boys and girls, peaceniks, in surplus military clothes, field jackets with infantry insignias on the shoulders, camouflage colors on paratrooper jackets and pants. Maybe it was a love-hate relationship.

I went into a bar where a slim girl was stroking a golden pole and jaded men bought overpriced drinks. She stroked the pole with nothing on, balls-assed naked with the cheeks of her ass soft and suede as her high-heeled boots. For the finale she walked the top of the bar, stopping once or twice to wiggle in some customer's face. The drinks were all the same . . . two fifty for a single shot, a beer, or a coke.

I wandered down Turk Street and picked up a pint of Yellowstone, a sour-mashed bourbon that old gang bosses loved to drink. I had a slug in an alley and shoved it into the inner pocket of my sport jacket. A drizzle began to fall. I had to get hold of a raincoat if I intended to wander around all night. I saw some lights . . . The Erogenous Zone. It cost five bucks and the show was live. I went in.

It wasn't a cabaret show with comedians and magicians and ventriloquists and a live band, only a topless bottomless show but much further out. The girls used dildos on each other and sucked each others' pussies on stage. I had never seen this sort of stuff before, not in the States. Maybe in Panama or Havana before Castro, but never in good old Catholic San Francisco, where they love the Forty-Niners and the Giants. It won't be long before we'll have a lady mayor, and that will be the end. My god. Three-quarters drunk with a dead girl in my apartment. More than a dead girl, my wife, and a love affair that wouldn't quit as long as it lasted. Then the girls came off the stage and sat on the laps of the men in the audience. For a few bucks in tips they squirmed on their laps, and the more aggressive girls helped a little with their hands. One girl sat on my lap. I gave her a small tip. I was there to kill time and needed money for the night, not for make-believe sex. I expected to stay put all night and listen to the canned tinny music and watch a parade of lovelies. Watch all the girls scooting across the laps of the men clutching dollar bills in their grubby hands. I had the image of a sex factory. I'd doze off for a few minutes and then startle awake and go into the can and take a slug of Yellowstone and then back to the seat.

I thought I had gone into an all-night show. I didn't want to go out on Market Street and see Mickey Mouse movies and cartoons until the wee hours . . . or horror films. I had had enough horror. But they hustled us out of the self-contained sex factory, and I was once again on the dark street. The rain had stopped, though the wind had come up. I walked briskly through the Tenderloin and hit the bars—the High Note and then Lynche's on Jones Street. In one bar on Geary two men, one after the other, showed me pieces. I asked, "Why is everyone packing guns?" They said that you needed a gun or a piece in the bars in this part of town. I wasn't going back to my place and disturb the dead to bring the .38 down just to drink.

Walking, walking along the Embarcadero with the masts of a few ships still visible and the railroad cars poised for the morning. The Sante Fe and the Southern Pacific and ahead on the track where I crossed the street the emblem on the side of a freight car, "The Route of Phoebe Snow." One ship, the passenger ship *Oriana*, at Pier Thirty-five with the lights on. I hung around talking to no one in particular, trying to decide if I wanted to go inside the shed and bother the guys loading stores and cargo or wait until the ship took on passengers in the morning.

I saw some pickets in front of the pier. I didn't know what was going on—and I didn't want to know. I had troubles of my own. They had stopped using Pier Thirty-seven, and Pier Thirty-nine was dark. The rumors being that this side of the Ferry Building was going condominium. All the real estate men dripping saliva to get their hands on a marine view. They'd sell marine views like hotcakes. What a long-winded conversation with myself to keep the images of the room and Sandy with a bullet hole in her belly and the blood coagulating by now and her body stiff and cold.

I stumbled along and made Sabella Latores and Borrusos next door, but I didn't linger in either place as I was in a hurry walking and waiting for the dawn. I knew that I had to go to Saint Mary's Cathedral and say my prayers and decide what to do. I veered across town toward North Beach, and as it started to drizzle again, I walked into a restaurant and picked up a raincoat folded over a chair. Just like that. I stole a raincoat. Not my usual way of doing things. I never considered myself a thief. But I needed the coat, and if I was caught, it was nothing compared to the troubles back in the room. I went into a Chinese grocery store and bought a quart of gin that fit slick and nice into the deep pockets of the raincoat.

The drizzle wet my hair as I stood outside the Condor. It was almost two in the morning, quitting time. I'd have to find a coffee shop that stayed open all night. I thought of Foster's Cafeteria on Geary and Van Ness. It had coffee and crowds of night people reading newspapers and waiting for the dawn. That Foster's was a long way from North Beach where I had copped the coat, and I noticed it was a good coat with a lining and not one rip.

I sat in Foster's rearranging my story and rearranging the body and checking the judge and jury. My one lawyer friend who had kept me solvent and out of jail with the 502s I had and all the cars I had wrecked and all the checks I had bounced. The time I left a Mustang on the freeway—a pretty good car just slammed into a retaining wall. It wouldn't start anymore, and I left it there. It was a stolen car at that, and he got me out of jail. Hinting at my character and steady line of work, he convinced the jury that I was really a responsible citizen who had a few problems with booze. He was good at picking juries. But he had one fault. He never picked a man for a jury who wore sunglasses. He was firm on this point, because he read in a legal journal the modern psychological interpretation—that people wore sunglasses to disguise a criminal or dark persona, that they had something to hide and were insecure and had a tendency to stick it to a defendant.

Even in Foster's I saw his eyebrows raise and the way he tugged on his suspenders. Well, I had a hell of a story to tell him about a dead wife and my fingerprints all over the gun. I still worried about that. I wasn't yet feeling remorse for Sandy, the poor kid from the wrong side of the Bighorn Mountains, the Sheridan County Kid. Wasn't she related to Wild Bill Hickok, buried in a boothill grave near Deadwood and not in some cheap apartment above a liquor store?

I looked through all the newspapers I scrounged and an old *Time* magazine someone had left. I read until my eyes blurred from the booze. I hadn't brought my reading glasses, but I had enough good sense not to be out in the lonely, deadly night. Much harder to push back the memories of Sandy and all the game playing with all the sex and the wine and candlelight and the long walks checking out the Victorian houses. Sunnyside, Congo Street, and the flower dance we put on by the glass-covered arboretum near her old neighborhood, the Haight District. Her old stomping ground, with all the buggy dipsos and addicts and flower children and diggers and hearses that they drove for fun—like the one with a cello sticking out the back. They fucked up the streets, and the streets were garbage. They fucked up all the old Victorian houses until they were so dirty that all the Filipinos and Blacks took a hike and left the goddam neighborhood to the pimps and the hustlers and the hangers-on.

The cafeteria crowd thinned out a few hours before dawn. I kept making runs to the shithouse, drinking shots of booze in paper cups of tea, as I didn't like gin and coffee. If I had a second chance, I'd buy a good bourbon and use it with coffee. By now my mouth tasted bitter, with a raspy roughness on the roof of my mouth from the three or four packs of cigarettes I had smoked. I went outside and searched for the dawn, looking up and down Van Ness Avenue. I went back in and asked if they had any cigars. They didn't. I tried the cigarette machine. Just the way I change booze, I changed to Tareytons. Killing myself with stale tobacco and juniper-berry booze, waiting for the light of day.

I was so fucked up and dreary and mind-boggled and fearful

and unstable and unsure. I had never been in a hole so deep—to find someone I cared for and loved and have her love me and then in some strange erratic chain of events have her dead. I knew no one would believe she shot herself. I didn't believe it until her hole-drilled body slumped to the floor. I still thought I'd resurrect our love and have a truce and then the walks and the dances in the sun and the sex-ridden nights would return, and I'd have hope again and something to work for and live for instead of rotgut and whiskey.

I knew they had a morning mass, as sure as Nixon was president, and they would open before five thirty and I'd go in and make my peace with Saint Mary. I washed my face, took another stiff slug, and waited with the old men and old women and even a cab driver for the mass and the blessings.

The high-vaulted cathedral. The Stations of the Cross. The kneeling supplicants. *We are all sinners.* The three-quarters-gone bottle of gin deep in the side pocket of the raincoat. I lit two candles and knelt before the small altar beside the main one, the liturgies in my ears.

Dear Saint Mary . . . watch over Sandy and forgive her for all her sins . . . forgive mine, too, but mainly dear Mother of God watch over her.

I read the inscription.

Our Mother of God
Listen my son, to what I tell you now:
Do not be troubled nor disturbed by anything;
Do not fear illness nor any distressing occurrence, nor pain.
Am I not your mother? Am I not life and health?
Have I not placed you on my lap and made you
my responsibility? Do you need anything else?

Dear Mother, keep me safe from the dark of the grave and make me walk in the light. May I meet my love where all children meet. May I be faithful to the image of my girl Rosalinda and my brother Monte. Most of all dear Mother . . . please take care of the soul of the poor young girl . . . Please Saint Mary make me walk beside her and not walk alone.

I was unable to stop the tears.

By the time I got back to my neighborhood the banks were open. I drew money out of the bank without looking at the place. The street was calm, not many people walking. Just everyday traffic, no ambulances, no police sirens, and no indication that Sandy was upstairs and dead. I crossed over to Hakk's to have another drink.

"Where'd you get that spiffy raincoat?" Milton asked. We knew each other from the bar. He had something to do with refrigeration. I ignored him and ignored the remark.

"Give the house a drink," I said.

"Must have hit a hot horse," Milton said.

He kept hoisting his drink to me. "Please, Milton, I've got a screeching headache." I did. Along with the pain in my gut. The trip to the church for consolation and direction had failed. I had run out of gas spiritually and emotionally. I had thought of taking all the money out of the bank and going to Canada with the rest of the nuts. The drinks went right through me. Down the hatch again, and there was no reprieve. I wasn't staggering, but I had gotten cut down and weary trying to hide my body in the raincoat. The sun dazzled the sidewalk outside Hakk's. I didn't know if I'd spend another night walking and dragging my ass across the city. I was running out of real estate unless I made the same circle. I asked Hakk to call me a cab.

The atmosphere at the Eagle Cafe was much more charged. Where were all the longshoremen? I said hello to Gunner, an old-timer from the Hill, and Dynamite, who leaned against the wall in a spot he always staked out for himself. I didn't remember if he was retired or on disability or drinking out a flop. Shot and a beer. I ordered a round for the entire bar. Some people at a table asked, "How 'bout us?" I told Lou to give them a drink. I sat mute, not talking, and once more I bought a drink for everyone. As the morning turned to afternoon, I began to feel I had to make a decision, but the decision had already been made.

At Fort Point, with the sunlight sparkling on the water, I threw the raincoat beyond the rocks and watched it float away. The surge of the waves carried it a little farther each time, until it reached the deeper blue of the channel. Then it raced with the incoming tide. Sea gulls made their dips near the edge of the channel. Pelicans nearby, but out of the way of an oil tanker coming under the bridge. I sat there smoking, not drinking, though I still had the pint of Yellowstone in my jacket pocket. Once I took the pint out, turned the cap, then changed my mind and shoved the pint into the paper bag and back into my pocket. I sat on the pilings watching—what? The old army fort. I had seen it many times and had fished off the rocks at the lower end. Casting into the swirls and eddies of water under the bridge.

I walked slowly toward Crissy Field and came out in the Marina. My feet were leaden. I had had enough. I called a cab and said Clement Street. Sick and tired of being sick and tired. Fucked up from drinking and disgusted with a life of downs and bad surprises and very few ups.

Swinging the bedroom door open. Body still there. What did I expect? The blanket over her face. I went in and lifted the blanket. What I saw wasn't Sandy but a twisted and stiff face. Blotches of blue around the cheeks. I covered her face again. The .38 was on the bed. I took it into the other room with me, sat in the chair by the telephone with the Yellowstone.

Rosalinda had surely called. I paced back and forth, then dialed the phone.

"Father, where were you? I called earlier."

"Rosalinda. Don't come up here, but send Monte. Be sure to tell him it's all an accident. It's all an error. That Sandy's was an accident."

"Sandy—what? What kind of accident? Are you all right?"

"I can't talk anymore." I hung up the phone. I knew she'd call right back.

I went into the room and pulled the blanket off Sandy. I didn't look at her. I rolled the pistol in my hand, spinning the barrel. Only one shell was gone.

It wasn't any attempt at Russian roulette. I saw the empty chamber clearly, and it was on the side.

XIV *Between the Circus and the Cemetery*

The wake and the funeral were successful. Everyone who was anyone along the docks showed up, especially since the men were on strike and the port was shut down. The one exception was the Old Man, but Monte had never seen him at a Catholic wake.

Monte handled Joe's funeral at an old-line parlor on Valencia Street. Because he shot himself in the temple and the bullet had come out through the eye and the nose, it was a closed-coffin funeral.

Monte tried not to be puzzled by the events. Joe killed himself, clear-cut suicide. But why had Sandy been shot? For what reason? And she had been dead for a much longer time. You didn't need a medical degree to see that. Monte found it impossible and impractical to speculate after the fact.

Sandy was cremated. Monte had called Wyoming, New Mexico, Hollywood, Beverly Hills. All he had was her maiden name, Bonner. Stabs in the dark. Nothing. Not knowing her religion, Monte, being the next of kin, knew what he had to do. He had her cremated.

Earlier, on the morning of his death, Joe was seen in the Eagle Cafe acting goofy, buying everyone drinks. But instead of talking and joking, he sat in the corner by himself. Monte knew Joe and all his actions. Drinking. Staying at the end of the bar meditating . . . contemplating. To blow one's brains out because of a two-bit whore? It wasn't logical. Just after establishing a relationship with his own daughter, his only child? Monte tried to comprehend, but nothing was there to grab. The only ones who could possibly know were dead. Slate wiped clean.

The union helped with the funeral and the burial, a deluxe coffin and a large, grand room for the wake. All the longshoremen and wives Monte had not seen in years. Some wives had grown older and fatter, but many seemed to retain part of their youth and had even become slimmer. Joe's friends and Monte's friends, all persuasions. Rosalinda's betrothed came from Bakersfield. Maria Teresa sent a wreath but didn't come. Monte in a dark suit outside Saint Philip's directing and talking and greeting. After the mass, the pallbearers—Roger, Sweetdick, Siberia Sam, Borrego Red, Zack, and Eddie Tijera. The Duke of Cream Sherry carrying all of Joe's cargo hooks in a plastic bag to be thrown atop the coffin later. Nanakule John, paralyzed and immobile, still in Kaiser Hospital.

Joe was buried in the National Cemetery to the side of Highway 101 near Rollingwood, not far from the old Tanforan racetrack that had recently burned down. The litany between the black-robed priest and the chaplain, at either end of the coffin, the flag-draped coffin resting on the metal frame with the soft rollers. The final blessing. The lowering of the casket. The American flag and the servicemen shooting their rifles. Tears in everyone's eyes. Monte brushed away his tears. The flag on the casket and the shooting of the rifles will do it every time, he decided. He saw the Duke swing his arm, and the plastic bag with the cargo hooks went into the grave beside the coffin.

Monte felt satisfied. He had orchestrated the whole scenario, the entire setting indelible. Slate gray sky, the threat of rain overhead but not a drop during the prayers at the burial site. Nature held in abeyance and the large crowd and the many cars. Monte didn't try for sympathy. He was too smart for that. Neither did he discourage it. He allowed himself to be cloaked in the veiled mystery of his brother's death.

After the burial the entourage went for a big feed at the Dovre Club in the Mission District. Monte went all out in a grand style. Some stopped on the way to calm their nerves at Coattail Molloy's across from Woodlawn Cemetery in Colma.

Rosalinda stayed near Monte. "Uncle Monte, you did well. It was a thoughtful and sincere service." As she talked he saw the Bible held tightly in her hands. It hadn't entered his mind to consult her about the mass and the burial. "I'm not staying for the get-together. Paul and I are driving back to the valley today." She stood very erect and tall, her dark hair covered by a white lace net.

"Did you know what happened?" Monte asked.

Rosalinda turned even paler than she had been. She looked alarmed.

"I don't know what happened. My dad called me up and said Sandy had an accident. To call you and for me not to come up. I called back again, but there was no answer. I hope I didn't start this trouble."

Monte kissed her on the cheek and he shook Paul's hand. "I'll be down for the wedding," Monte said. "I'm good for a smashing gift."

Monte watched them walk away. Now he had to concentrate on the pickets and the strike.

About the Author

George Benet is an anomaly. He has a master's degree in English, but he has just retired as a longshoreman after twenty-seven years on the docks of San Francisco and Oakland. As a writer, he has been proclaimed by Marxists to be an authentic voice of the proletariat, but he is a Roman Catholic who votes the Democratic ticket. He's an alcoholic who is a writing junkie. Benet says: "I have no market profile. My readers are stockbrokers, academics, waitresses, nurses, longshoremen, racetrack handicappers, hookers. I write for the working stiff, the street corner hustler, the outlaw, the off-track bettor. Writing is not a mystery or myth or therapy for me. Writing is a simple way for me to touch another human being."

Benet was born and raised in Chicago, and served in the Navy during World War II. He was widowed once, divorced once and has two children. A Research Associate for the Institute for the Study of Social Change at UC Berkeley, Benet writes papers of a sociological nature for them on such topics as the effect of mechanization and automation on the maritime industry, the counterculture, and call girls and prostitutes.

Benet is the author of *A Place in Colusa*, published by Singlejack Books in San Pedro, and is included in *The Waterfront Writers*, published by Harper and Row. A much-published poet, Benet also has many articles and short stories to his credit. He lives in the Richmond District of San Francisco.